BREAKING POINT

DELTA FORCE STRONG
BOOK SEVEN

ELLE JAMES

TWISTED PAGE INC

BREAKING POINT

DELTA FORCE STRONG BOOK #7

New York Times & *USA Today*
Bestselling Author

ELLE JAMES

EBOOK ISBN: 978-1-62695-364-2

PRINT ISBN: 978-1-62695-365-9

Dedicated to Megan and Cleve for running interference
while I worked under an impossible deadline.
Go Team!

AUTHOR'S NOTE

Enjoy other military books by Elle James

Visit ellejames.com for titles and release dates
For hot cowboys, visit her alter ego Myla Jackson at
mylajackson.com
and join Elle James's Newsletter at
https://ellejames.com/contact/

CHAPTER 1

JOHN "TANK" Sanders adjusted the septic line to his shiny silver Airstream camp trailer. If the contractor had finished building the house on his property when he was supposed to, John wouldn't have had to resort to living in his recreational vehicle for the final two months of construction. But he'd already given notice to his apartment complex, packed all the stuff he cared about and sold the rest. Not that he had much. Living in apartments, transferring from post to post and being deployed as a US Army Delta Force operator, kept him from accumulating too much junk. A few photographs, a collection of vinyl records, his favorite easy chair, an assortment of fishing tackle and a few other items, had been relegated to a storage unit for the time being.

Not having much meant he'd start from scratch

furnishing his new home. That would be expensive. He snorted softly. As if the entire building process hadn't been expensive to begin with. It irritated him to no end that he could easily have performed a majority of the construction himself.

If he wasn't on call to be deployed.

As a teen, he'd worked in construction during the summers, framing houses, laying tile, roofing buildings and more. He could have done everything except the concrete work. However, he preferred to let the plumbers lay in the pipes and the electricians the wiring. Some things were better left to those with a lot more experience than he had in those areas.

As he washed his hands beneath the water hose, a commotion caught his attention.

"Hey!" a young man shouted.

Tank dropped the hose and spun.

Four guys dressed in black T-shirts and black cargo pants with the waistbands resting low enough to display four inches of boxer shorts, circled a teenaged girl with auburn hair, refusing to let her out of their control. A tall, thin young man with dark hair and a pale complexion tried to push his way through the guys to get to the girl.

"She's too pretty for a geek like you." A guy with a nose ring and a spike piercing through his eyebrow lifted a lock of auburn hair and sniffed it. "Mmm, and she smells good."

The girl jerked her head away and spit at the young man. "Back off, jerk face."

Piercing Guy stepped toward her, raising his fists. "Why you—"

The tall thin teen lunged toward him. "Leave her alone!"

"Or what?" The biggest of the dudes in black shirts shoved the thin guy so hard he staggered backward.

Once he steadied, the thin man stood out of range of the bully's hands, his brow furrowing. "Or...or I'll call the police."

"Go ahead. By the time they get here, we'll be gone," the bully said. "With your girlfriend."

"She's not my girlfriend," the young man said. "She's my friend."

"In that case, she'll be *my* girlfriend." The bully slipped his arm around the auburn-haired girl's shoulder.

The young woman snorted. "Like hell." She jabbed her elbow hard into the bully's side, ducked out from beneath his arm and stepped away from the circle of guys in black.

Tank nearly laughed at how quickly the girl escaped her tormentors. He wanted to shout, *good for you*, but stayed out of it. He didn't like to get involved unless he absolutely had to. In the back of his mind, he knew he'd have to do something to de-escalate the tension between the bullies and the other two young people. However, he really hoped they'd sort it out before he had to intervene.

"Bitch." The bully lunged toward the girl.

Tank closed the distance between himself and the group in four long strides and came to a stop between the thin man and the girl. He crossed his arms over his chest and faced off with the leader of the group of bullies.

The big guy stood tall, coming a couple inches short of Tank's six foot three inches.

Tank tipped his head back slightly and stared down his nose at the thug. "You live around here?"

"Maybe we do," the bully said, his eyes narrowing as if daring anyone to dispute.

"Do they?" Tank asked.

The girl shook her head. "No."

Tank braced his feet, raised his chin just a bit more and said, "Leave."

"You can't tell us what to do," Piercing Guy said, standing a few steps behind his leader.

Tank wasn't worried about the guy with the piercings. It wouldn't take much to put him in his place. He wasn't really worried about the bully either. Bullies usually took advantage of their size to intimidate.

Tank used his head. Size only went so far in a fight. Cunning and skill made the difference in whether you won or lost. Tank had the skills. He'd bet his favorite knife the bully only knew how to throw punches, not how to aim for effectiveness.

"Stay out of it, old man," the big bully said.

Heat rose up Tank's neck into his head. He tamped down the flash of anger, refusing to let the younger man know his words had hit a sore spot. Hell, it shouldn't be a sore spot. Not every Delta lived through some of their missions. Being older meant he'd escaped death on a number of occasions. He'd even begun to dream about retiring from the military in four short years. He tried not to think about it. A lot could happen in four years. He didn't want to jinx himself. "Just leave."

The bully stepped closer. "You gonna make me?"

Tank drew in a deep breath and let it out through his nose. "Yeah."

The big guy motioned Tank forward with a sneer and a lift of his chin. "Bring it."

Tank shook his head. "You don't want this."

"No?" Bully snorted. "Try me." His buddies gathered around him, ready to make the odds four-to-one.

Again, Tank shook his head. "I don't want to hurt anyone."

The bully's bark of laughter did little to shake Tank's confidence. "The only one who's gonna get hurt is you, old man." He tipped his head toward Tank. "Let's do this." As he moved forward, his followers moved with him, surrounding Tank.

Tank stood his ground. If they wanted a piece of him, they'd have to take the first swing.

"Call 9-1-1," the girl urged the tall skinny guy. She dove for a rotting two-by-four board lying on the ground beneath the trailer beside her. When she straightened, she ran to stand beside Tank.

Tank blocked her from passing him. "Stay back."

She frowned. "They're going to cream you." With both hands gripping the board, she faced the gang with her lips pulled back in a fierce snarl.

She was cute in her fierceness…but the board was rotted and wouldn't hold up long enough to help. "I've got this," he assured her. "I don't want to worry about you getting caught in the crossfire."

"But…" she started, her eyebrows dipping.

The young, thin man gripped her arm and pulled her back several steps. "I've notified the police," he said quietly.

"That's right, chicken shit," the bully called out to the thin young man. "Hide behind your girlfriend."

"Shut up," the girl said.

"You think you're so tough now that you have someone else to stick up for you?" The bully raised his fists and took a swing at Tank.

Tank was ready. He caught the fist in his palm. The force behind the swing made his hand hurt. A little. He wrapped his hand around the man's fist, pushed the hand down, snagged his wrist and spun him around. Then he jacked the man's arm up between his shoulder blades until the bully screamed like a girl.

The sound gave Tank a small measure of satisfaction.

The bully's friends stood a few feet away, their eyes wide.

Tank stared at them between slitted eyes and whispered, "Boo."

The other three gang members backed away so fast, one fell on his ass.

Tank would've laughed, but he couldn't. The man he held with his arm up his back squirmed.

"Let go of me," he demanded.

"Not until you apologize to the lady and her boyfriend for being mean to them," Tank demanded.

The bully snorted. "Fuck you and fuck her."

Tank leaned close to the man's ear. "Now, you'll have to apologize for your language as well." He increased the pressure on the man's arm until the bully stood on his tiptoes, his face breaking out in a sweat.

"Okay, okay," he cried. "I apologize."

Still holding tightly onto the man's arm, Tank refused to relent. "For what?"

"For being mean and cussing." He threw his head back. "Let go!"

Tank gave the man a shove, sending him flying forward. He landed on his hands and knees in the dust.

When he pushed to his feet, he spun to face Tank and pulled a gun from the pocket of his hoodie. "You aren't so commanding now, are you?"

Tank's eyes narrowed to slits. "You better make your first shot count. You won't get a second."

The pierced guy shook his head. "Look, Sly, I ain't getting involved in no gun fight. Neither should you."

"Shut up, Bodie," Sly said. "You're as much of a chicken shit as Alston is." The bully tipped his head toward the tall skinny dude.

"Think-twice before you shoot," a woman's voice sounded behind the bully.

All eyes turned toward the sound.

Tank stared at an older version of the girl who could have been her sister, but he guessed was her mother. She held a pistol in her hand, aimed at the bully. Her hand was steady, her jaw set in a firm line. The fierce expression in her eyes, the way she stood with her feet slightly apart and her shoulders thrown back made Tank's groin tighten. She was like a Valkyrie bent on slaying the enemy. Or a mother bear willing to take on a pack of wolves to save her cub.

Sly snorted and turned his weapon toward the woman. "You won't shoot."

Her eyes narrowed into slits of green. "Try me." Her pretty lips pressed into a thin line, and her hand remained steady, her gun aimed at Sly's chest. "The question is whose bullet will leave the gun first?"

For a long moment, Sly stared at the woman, his

cheeks a ruddy red, his lip curled back in a feral snarl. Finally, he tucked his gun into the pocket of his hoodie and turned to Ryan, the skinny guy. "Tell your brother he owes us. And I collect on my debts." With a quick jerk of his head toward the others in his group, Sly led the way back to their motorcycles. He straddled a black Harley with a devil's head and purple flames painted on the fuel tank.

The other guys rode a variety of motorcycles, none as fancy or expensive as Sly's. Once they started the engines, they revved them loudly then spun out in the gravel, leaving a trail of Texas dust in their wake.

Still holding her gun pointed at the leader of the pack, the woman watched until the four motorcycles disappeared out of the trailer park. When they were gone, she lowered her weapon, let go of a long shaky breath and turned back to Tank. "Thank you," she said.

He shrugged. "I didn't do anything." Tank nodded toward the gun in her hand. "You had all the incentive they needed. How experienced are you with that?"

She laughed. "Not a bit. I'm not even sure there's a bullet chambered."

"Do you mind?" Tank held out his hand.

"Sure. I bought it when we moved into the park." She turned the gun around and handed it to him by the handle. "I haven't had time to go to the range and practice."

He ejected the magazine from the handle, a sinking feeling hitting him low in the belly. The magazine was empty, as was the gun. "These aren't effective if you don't put bullets in them."

Her lips twisted in a wry grin. "I've had it a month. This is the first time I took it out of the box it came in. I do have bullets, but I guess they're still in the box." She shrugged. "At least it got the point across."

Tank inserted the magazine into the handle, checked the safety switch and handed the gun back to her. "You should make time to go to the range, in case those guys decide to come back. They might not fall for your bluff a second time."

She sighed and shifted the gun to her other hand. "I'm Collette McCallick."

He wrapped his fingers around hers and felt their warmth. "John Sanders." A shock of awareness blasted through his veins at the feel of her smooth skin against his calluses.

Collette lifted her chin toward his camp trailer. "Staying long?"

He shrugged. "As long as it takes for the contractors to finish building my house. They're a couple of months behind, and my apartment lease was up."

The woman gave a brief smile. "Nice that you had

a choice and don't have to move into a hotel for that timeframe."

"Yeah." He looked toward the single-wide mobile home the woman's daughter stood beside. "How long are you here?"

Her gaze went to the trailer that had seen better days. The paint was faded, and the wooden porch was so weathered it needed several boards replaced, and the railing was hanging uselessly in one place. "This is home." Her gaze returned to his. "At least for the next year."

"A year?"

"That's how long it'll take for me to get through the rest of my education."

Not normally one to strike up a conversation with a stranger, Tank couldn't help asking, "Education?"

"I'm studying to be a nurse." She sighed. "And I really should get back to my books. I have a test tomorrow. Thanks again. And welcome to the park. Sorry it isn't so friendly." She gave him a crooked grin and fell in step behind the younger version of herself and the teenaged boy climbing up the rickety wooden stairs to the trailer.

Tank's gaze followed the trio, his attention lingering on the pretty mother of the teen. She didn't look to be much more than a teen herself. Except for some very fine lines around her eyes, she looked as fresh-faced as her daughter.

Collette turned in the doorframe and glanced back to where he stood. A pretty, pink blush filled her cheeks. She entered the trailer and shut the door. When the latch didn't engage, she opened and closed it a second time. Again, it wouldn't close all the way. Finally, she slammed the door hard, and the latch held.

His first day in the trailer park, and he'd already set up his trailer, hooked up the water and septic lines, broken up a fight and rescued a couple of women being threatened by a motorcycle gang. Being in a trailer park hadn't been his idea, but the campgrounds were filled with summer travelers, and they were too expensive for the two months he had to wait for the construction crews to finish his house. For two months, he should be able to put up with anything.

And if a woman and her daughter could survive in the park, he could, too.

He frowned, his gaze on the closed door. He wasn't convinced the mother and daughter were all that safe. If the motorcycle gang returned, they could easily overtake the pretty little redhead and her gorgeous mother. After being humiliated at the point of a gun, the gang might decide to return to exact their revenge.

Images of drive-by shootings and Molotov cocktails flashed through Tank's mind. If those thugs decided they didn't like how someone had threatened them, they could come back and cause a whole lot of trouble.

Shoving the woman's dilemma to the back of his mind, he double-checked the electric, water and sewer lines. Satisfied they were all functioning appropriately, he entered his tiny as hell trailer and closed the screen door, leaving the metal door open.

With a frustrated sigh, he glanced around the small interior of the camp trailer and prayed the building contractor made up for lost time and shortened the two months into less than a month. He had so looked forward to having his house complete on his own little piece of heaven, a two-hundred-acre ranch just outside of Copperas Cove. Far enough away from Fort Hood that he didn't have to smell the diesel from the military vehicles, and close enough he could get to work within thirty to forty minutes, depending on traffic.

He'd saved his money for the sixteen years he'd been in the Army with the intention of retiring to a ranch where he'd raise cows, ride horses and find a job selling insurance or real estate. Definitely something with a lesser likelihood of being some enemy combatant's target practice. As a Delta Force operator, he'd been shot several times, had shrapnel dug out of his body and had concussions from explosive blasts several times. He's survived a helicopter crash, terrorist attacks, improvised explosive devices and more. He looked forward to the peace and quiet of the hot Texas countryside with the smell of dust, horse manure and mesquite trees, instead of aviation or diesel fuel.

Four more years, and he could retire. Until then, he belonged to the Army, and he served with pride. The house and ranch...they were his future.

If he lived long enough to enjoy it.

With the fighting arena constantly shifting, he never knew where he'd land. Eventually, he'd come back to his ranch in Texas. And his home would be waiting. Well...as soon as the contractor finished building it.

In the meantime, he was stuck in a trailer he'd only planned on using for fishing and hunting trips. Short fishing and hunting trips. Not camping for two months.

At least his neighbor seemed nice enough. His thoughts went to the pretty redhead with her mini-me daughter. Tank wondered where her husband was and what he did for a living that kept them in a single-wide mobile home in a trailer park. Their daughter had to be at least sixteen.

He grinned as an image of the mother holding a handgun came to mind.

The older Ms. McCallick had a lot of guts to pull an empty gun on a thug like Sly.

His grin faded. Thankfully, Sly hadn't tested her trigger finger reaction time or she'd be dead. His hands tightened into fists. He shouldn't have let go of

Sly when he had. At the very least, he should've frisked him for weapons before he had. Hell, he should have called the cops. The problem with calling the cops was, that by the time they would have arrived, the gang would have been long gone.

Tank opened the refrigerator and stared at the mostly empty shelves. All he had were a couple of steaks he'd rescued from his freezer before closing the door to his apartment for the last time. They were thawed and needed to be grilled. But that was all he had. He needed to shop for groceries, but after moving his stuff from his apartment to a storage unit, and then setting up the trailer in the park, he was hot, tired and didn't feel like facing a store full of people in a hurry to get home.

John stepped outside to the outdoor grill, doused the charcoal briquets with lighter fluid and threw a lit match on it. He went back inside grabbed a beer from the fridge, twisted off the cap and took a long swig. He had just settled onto faux-leather sofa, that happened to also have a bed hidden beneath its cushions, when a loud knock sounded on his door.

Tank rose from his seat, set the beer on the counter and pushed the door open.

The younger McCallick stood at the base of his metal stairs, her eyes round and her gaze darting from him back to the trailer she lived in. "You gotta come quick. My mom needs you." Without bothering to explain, the young woman raced back to the trailer.

With the motorcycle gang fresh on his mind, Tank leaped through the door, skipping the steps altogether, and hit the ground running.

CHAPTER 2

COLLETTE STOOD in front of the kitchen sink, holding a skillet lid up like a shield as water spewed from the faucet, soaking her from head to toe and everything else in the kitchen. Exhausted from a full day of studying and tests, followed by four hours on her feet as a waitress at the Salty Dog Saloon, she just couldn't clear her head long enough to figure out how to make the water stop gushing in her face.

Somewhere in her peripheral vision, she was aware her daughter, Hope, had left the trailer. She probably hadn't wanted to drown in the spray from the broken faucet. Collette worried she'd be outside and cornered by the returning motorcycle gang. She was just about to leave the deluge and go find her daughter when Hope burst through the door. "Help is on its way," she called out.

A second behind her daughter, the doorway

filled with the massive shoulders and tall form of the man who'd come to her daughter's rescue earlier.

He took one look at the spewing faucet hardware and dove past her ankles to the doors beneath the sink. Flinging them open, he stuck his head inside, reached his arm in, twisted something and the shower fizzled to a trickle and finally stopped.

Collette lowered the lid and stared around at the kitchen covered in water, their dinner of tuna sandwiches ruined. Tears mixed with the droplets of water and slipped down her cheeks.

The man...what was his name?...John...pulled his head out from under the counter and rolled to his feet. His massive form filled the small kitchen, overpowering Collette's senses.

She backed up so fast, and her feet slipped on the wet floor. Flinging out her arms, she clocked John with the pan lid and tipped backward, losing her balance.

As if in slow motion, she fell.

A hand reached out and snagged her empty one, yanking her forward to slam against a chest so rock-solid it knocked the breath out of her. Or was she breathless because he was so strong and vital and... holy moly...masculine?

With one hand holding his and the other still clinging to the skillet lid, she stared up into the man's brown-black eyes and noted his chiseled features and sexy lips. Her heart beat faster, and her breathing became even more erratic.

"Are you okay?"

Was she? Collette blinked and reminded herself to breathe. She nodded, still pressed against his chest.

"We got towels." Hope hurried into the kitchen followed by Ryan, each possibly carrying every towel they owned. And it would take all of them to sop up the water.

"We'd better dry the floors before the water damages the subfloors," John said.

Stupidly, Collette nodded. Then, as if finally coming to her senses, she pushed away from his body and stepped backward to grab a towel off the stack her daughter carried. "You're soaked," she said. "I'm so sorry. I'm sure this wasn't what you'd planned for your evening. You're probably getting settled in."

"It's okay. Let me help." He wiped his face with the towel then dropped it on the floor and squatted down to absorb the water until the towel was soaked.

Collette took another towel from her daughter, sank to her knees and worked beside the man who'd come to her rescue now twice in one day. "Thank you," she said. "I should've thought to shut off the water."

"When you're being blinded by the spray, it's hard to think straight." He rose, twisted the towel over the sink to wring the water out, and then bent to soak up more.

Collette did the same. Hope and her boyfriend, Ryan, helped as well. Soon, the kitchen floor was dry, and they used a couple of towels to dry the counters.

"Was this dinner?" Hope asked as she scooped the soggy sandwiches Collette had just made into the trash.

"Sadly, yes." Collette sighed. "That was the last of the tuna."

"That's okay," Hope said. "Ryan wanted to take me out for burgers anyway. Do you mind?" Her daughter waited for Collette's response, ever considerate of her mother, for which Collette was eternally grateful. Since Collette had decided to go back to school, Hope had been supportive of her efforts, taking on more responsibility in the home and not complaining when they'd had to downsize from the rent house to a single-wide mobile home to make the money work, while Collette went through her training to become a registered nurse. What little savings she'd managed to put aside and the wages she made working part time at the Salty Dog Saloon, plus the tips, helped Collette pay the bills, keep a roof over their heads and food on the table. But that was about it.

Though Hope was old enough to drive, they shared the old beater of a car between the two of them. More often than not, Hope rode her bicycle as often as she could. The juggling act to pick up and drop each other off was onerous and took a lot of coordination. Collette hated that she couldn't provide a better life for her daughter. When Hope had a chance to escape their dire circumstances, Collette was eager to let her. "Go enjoy," she said. "And thank you, Ryan." She smiled at the shy young man who'd become more and more a part of their little family. She frowned as she warned, "Watch out for that guy who was here earlier."

"Sly?" Hope shook her head. "He's nothing but a bully."

"A bully with a gun," Collette reminded her.

Hope nodded, her lips pressing into a line. "I hope he doesn't catch up to Ryan's brother."

"What did he mean by *he owes me?*" Collette asked.

Ryan's eyebrows drew together. "My brother hasn't always been smart about drugs. Apparently, Mark was buying them from Sly at one point. Then his best friend, Tyler, overdosed on some really bad stuff Sly had sold him." He shook his head. "After Tyler died, my brother changed. He quit the drugs cold-turkey and he tried to talk his other friends out of doing drugs. But as long as dealers supplied them, they weren't giving them up." Ryan glanced toward Hope. "He won't tell me what happened, but I think he took Sly's inventory."

"Stole it?" Collette asked.

Ryan nodded. "Yeah."

"Is he using again?" John asked.

"I don't think so," Ryan said. "Tyler's death hit him really hard. I think he's clean."

"What did he do with the drugs?" Collette asked.

"I don't know," Ryan said. "I think he might have flushed them."

John bent to sop up a small puddle of the water on the floor.

When he straightened, his shoulders seemed impossibly broad in the tight confines of Collette's trailer kitchen. With the drama of a broken faucet over, Collette really had time to study the man. And boy was he something.

He wore a white T-shirt that was stuck to his chest, accentuating those chiseled muscles.

Collette's mouth went dry, and her blood raced through her veins. She's never had such an intensely physical reaction to any man. At least not since she'd made love to Hope's biological father. Even then, her reaction to him hadn't been as visceral as the feeling she had standing there in front of John in his wet T-shirt.

Hope slapped another towel into Collette's hands.

Collette dragged her gaze away from the thickly corded muscles of John's chest and stared down at the towel in her hands, blinking.

Hope gave an exasperated sigh. "To dry off."

Collette glanced at John's wet chest.

"Well, we're leaving for burgers," Hope said. "Want anything?"

Collette turned toward her daughter. "No. I'm fine," she muttered.

Hope tipped her head toward the empty counter where the wet sandwiches had been. "Seriously, Mom?"

Collette shrugged. "I'll come up with something for dinner."

"Whatever, Mom." Hope backed for the door. "We'll be back in about an hour." She nodded her head toward John. "Thanks for helping."

"My pleasure," John said.

Hope's gaze returned to her mother. "You gonna be all right?"

Her pulse finally under control, Collette nodded. "I will be, once I clean up this mess."

Her daughter turned toward her boyfriend standing in the doorframe, waving a hand over her shoulder. "See ya later, Mom."

Ryan held the door open for her.

Hope paused on the threshold. "Oh, and Mom…" she shot a glance over her shoulder, one side of her mouth turned up, "FYI. You can see through your shirt." With her parting shot, Collette's daughter left the trailer.

Ryan closed the door behind them.

Collette looked down at her shirt and gasped, raising the towel to cover her chest. Her cheeks heated, and her gaze shot to John.

His lips twitched on the corners for a brief moment, but then he gripped her shoulders, spun her around behind him and let go. "I'll be right back."

Before she could form a thought or a sentence, John was out the trailer door, slamming it behind him.

Collette ran to her bedroom at the other end of the trailer, tore her wet T-shirt over her head and pulled on a dry rib-knit sleeveless sweater in a sea-foam green, peeled her jeans off and dragged on a pair of dry white shorts. As she zipped them, a knock sounded on her front door. She hurried to answer, finding John standing there with a small toolbox.

He gave her a twisted grin. "The water's off, but the faucet will spray again if you turn it on."

"Right." She opened the door wide, allowing him to enter. As he passed by her, she smoothed a hand over her damp hair, wishing she'd had the time to run a brush through the tangles. Not that she cared what this man thought about how she looked.

Well, maybe she did just a little.

John hadn't taken the time to change out of his wet clothes. With the fabric still plastered to his skin, he set the toolbox on the floor and extracted a screwdriver and a wrench from its depths, his biceps flexing, his denim jeans pulling taut over his tight…

He straightened, his gaze capturing hers staring at his ass.

Her cheeks heated. "Is there…anything…I can do for you?" she stammered. *Like take off your shirt and lick the moisture off your chest.* Just the thought skimming through her mind made her cheeks flush even hotter. "I mean, can I hold you…stuff. I meant stuff."

He chuckled. "Actually, you can hold the parts as I disassemble the faucet. I don't want them to get knocked down the drain or into the garbage disposal."

She nodded. "Sure." Though she wondered if she'd be any good at assisting. Her hands shook, and her knees wobbled. The kitchen seemed to get even smaller as he stood there, his shoulders blocking the light from the fixture over his head. The man was larger than life and too sexy for her, considering it had been a very long time since she'd been on a date, and even longer since she'd made love. Granted, she'd worn out a vibrator or two, but the actual physical touch of a man's hand on her body…

What would it be like to have John touch her with those big, callused hands of his?

Her heartbeat kicked up yet another notch until it was racing, slamming hard against her chest.

Collette drew in a deep breath and willed her pulse to calm. Nope. It wasn't happening. The longer she stood near him, the more she trembled.

Thankfully, John turned his back to her and went to work on the faucet. One by one, he handed her the pieces as he worked his way to the root of the problem. Each time he laid an item in her hand, his touch sparked a current of electricity that raced up her arm and throughout her body.

By the time he'd disassembled the entire faucet, Collette was a highly strung set of nerves ready to explode.

He held up a small round piece of rubber. "Thought so," he said. "The gasket is worn out."

"Oh," she said, for lack of anything intelligent to say when all she wanted to do was run her hands over his shoulders to see if his muscles were as hard as she suspected.

"Fortunately, I have a spare. I had to replace a gasket on the shower in my camper recently, and they came in packets of two." He rummaged through the toolkit until he found a small plastic bag with a black rubber circle like the broken one, only this one was intact. He quickly fit it in place, and then plucked one piece of the assembly at a time from her palms.

Within fifteen minutes, he had the faucet put together.

Collette doubted a plumber could have done it faster. And a plumber would've charged a lot of money just to come out. And if she'd called the owner of the trailer she rented, he'd have had to call a plumber. And who knew how long that would've taken?

"Let's see if it fixed the problem." He grinned, making butterflies flutter against the insides of Collette's belly. "You might want to get your shield ready."

Collette grabbed the pan lid and held it in front of

her, hoping the gasket worked and she'd remain dry. She braced herself, preparing for the worst.

John dropped to his knees, rolled onto his side and reached under the sink where he twisted the knobs, turning on the hot and cold water.

A moment or two passed and…nothing.

John pulled his head out from under the cabinet. "Turn on the faucet."

Collette leaned over him and turned on the water. It flowed just the way it was supposed to, no leakage, no explosions of water and no flooding her kitchen. She grinned. "How can I thank you?"

"By helping me up off the floor." He held out his hand.

She reached down, gripped his hand and leaned back, giving him enough leverage to roll to his feet.

When he did, he was so close their chests bumped.

Collette teetered backward on her heels.

"Whoa there." John slipped a hand around her, pulled her close and steadied her. "Are you all right?"

With him so near to her, she could barely catch her breath. Her hands rested against his chest. And yes, his muscles were every bit as hard as she'd imagined. "I'm okay." Still, she didn't move away. She stood as if paralyzed by her unexpected attraction to the man.

He raised his hand and brushed his thumb across her cheek. "You missed a spot."

She raised her hand, covering his with hers. "Did I?" What was wrong with her? She had a better vocabulary than that of an inexperienced schoolgirl.

"I got it," he said.

When there was nothing else to keep them standing there, Collette finally pulled herself together and stepped backward, letting her hands fall to her sides. She rubbed them against her shorts. "I'd offer you dinner for your trouble, but—"

"It got wet in the downpour," he finished. "How about this? I was about to throw some steaks on the grill. Why don't you come eat with me?"

She shook her head, frowning. "But you helped *me.* I owe *you* dinner."

"You can repay me with your company. You're the only person I know here, and I hate eating alone." He cocked an eyebrow. "Or am I too much of a stranger for you to feel comfortable?"

She laughed. "Considering we've gone swimming together, survived a flood and worked a project like a maintenance team, I'd say we're past the stranger stage." She held out her hand. "I'd love to join you for dinner. I might even have some salad fixings left in the refrigerator and a can of green beans."

"Good. I can cook a steak like a master chef, but I never remember to add vegetables to my meals."

"You really should." Collette shrugged. "Granted, canned green beans don't have the best nutritional value, but they're better than nothing." She reached around him to the cabinet over his left shoulder and retrieved the can of green beans, noting how few cans there were of anything. She really needed to make a trip to the grocery store or send Hope with a wad of her tip money. Whatever they got wouldn't be much, and it would have to last until she worked again the next weekend.

Her paychecks weren't large. They covered most of the monthly rent, but it was her tip money she relied on to pay for groceries, gas and books. Thankfully, her utilities were included in the rent. It was one of the reasons she'd chosen to move her and her daughter out of a decent rent house into this dump of a trailer. It was a set amount, unlike utilities in most places, which could fluctuate with the seasons. Her paycheck plus some money from her savings and her tips had to see them through the year and a half remaining for her to finish her training.

Collette's stomach knotted. "I'm due a trip to the store. There's not much room to store things in this little kitchen, which means I have to go buy groceries more often."

She quickly closed the cabinet door, embarrassed by the lack of food. The last thing she wanted was for this man to feel sorry for her or think she wasn't providing enough for her child. Her boss at the Salty Dog would let her work extra days if she needed the money. And it looked like she'd have to pick up another shift soon to help fill her refrigerator with enough food for two to make it another week.

John was frowning at the closed cabinet door. "Is that all the pantry staples you have?"

"It is for now. Again, I'm due a trip to the store."

His eyes narrowed as he stared into her face.

Collette's shoulders squared, and she lifted her chin, meeting his gaze without flinching. "Look, if you're planning on feeding me steak out of some sense of charity, you can eat alone. I have food. I'm not starving. And I can contribute a damned can of green beans and a salad to a meal."

He held up his hands like a shield. "Okay, okay. I was serious. I don't like to eat alone. You're the only friendly face I know in the trailer park." His lips twisted into a crooked smile. "Well, it *was* the only friendly face." He pointed at her mouth. "You're kind of frowning now."

When Collette realized she was scowling, she forced her face to relax and shook out the stiffness in her arms and shoulders. "Sorry. I didn't mean to be ungrateful."

"I don't need gratitude. I need greens." He winked and patted his flat belly. "Gotta stay healthy for my job."

She turned to the refrigerator and grabbed out what was left of a head of lettuce, half a tomato and a bottle of salad dressing. Fortunately, the lettuce and tomato still looked good. She tore off a wilted leaf, pulled out her cutting board and made quick work of cutting up a salad. "What do you do that requires you to stay healthy?" she asked over her shoulder.

"Army," he responded.

The hand holding the knife slipped, and she nicked her fingertip. "Ouch." She dropped the knife and stuck her finger beneath the water faucet he'd just fixed, running water over the small cut.

"Let me see." He gripped her shoulders and turned her to face him, taking her hand in his. "Do you have a paper towel or cloth?"

"No paper towels, but I have a dishtowel in the drawer beside you."

Still holding her hand in his larger one, he opened the drawer with the other hand and pulled out a clean towel, wrapped it around her finger and looked up. "Alcohol and bandages?"

Collette tipped her head toward her right shoulder. "Above the sink to my right."

He reached past her, his arm brushing her ear, sending waves of awareness through her. He smelled of wet male and the outdoors.

She inhaled, closing her eyes. She didn't want to admit she was feeling desire for this stranger. Awareness was enough to deal with. Desire equaled distraction. She didn't have the time or the energy for distraction. She had to get through her nursing course. She needed a good-paying job so that she could help Hope through college.

As he leaned toward the cabinet, their hands were sandwiched between them, his knuckles grazing her breasts, the back of her hand touching his chest.

Breathing became more difficult.

Finally, he came away with a small bottle of alcohol that had only a few drops left and an old box of bandages with cartoon figures decorating them. She was pretty sure they were some she'd purchased when Hope had been learning to walk and run.

He pulled one out, and the paper around it crumbled it was so old. John shook his head. Still holding her hand in his with the cloth wrapped tightly around her injured finger, he started for the door. "Come on. I have a first aid kit in my camper."

She dug in her heels. "It's okay. I'm sure the bleeding has already stopped. It's not like I cut off my finger. It's just a little cut."

"You're coming with me."

"But the salad—"

"Can wait. Besides, I'm not keen on blood on my lettuce." He winked. "Seriously, we can come back and get the salad and green beans after we bandage your wound."

"You're going to think I'm a lousy neighbor." Collette let him guide her toward the door. "What with broken faucets and poor cooking skills."

"I'm not thinking anything like that. I'm thinking I'm hungry enough to eat a side of beef, that my charcoal is getting hot and those steaks aren't going to cook themselves." He stopped at her door. "Now, are you going to let me get you to that first aid kit, or are you going to argue some more?"

"Your steak is calling." She pushed past him and led the way through the door. "Let's do this."

His chuckle behind her warmed her insides. He wasn't mad at her. He was hangry and ready for his dinner. She'd have dinner with him, and that would be the end of it.

She sighed.

Too bad he was in the Army. She'd sworn off military men when Hope's father had left Fort Hood without saying goodbye or kiss my ass. Three dates, and he hadn't even called or texted her to let her know he was joining the Army and had a reporting date. He hadn't cared enough to end whatever had just started. Collette had had to find out from one of his friends that he'd left. A couple months later, she'd called to let him know that she was pregnant with his child, but he hadn't even answered his phone.

She'd left a message.

No response.

She'd known he'd been taking calls and texts because his friends had still been communicating with him. He just hadn't wanted anything to do with her or his child.

Pregnant at sixteen, she'd kept it secret from her parents as long as she could. When they'd found out, they'd been livid. They'd allowed her to stay until she'd given birth. Then they'd set her up in apartment, gave her enough money to live on for three months and told her to deal with life.

Alone at seventeen, she'd had to find daycare for her baby, get a job and tough it out on her own.

She hadn't gone back to her parents for anything. They'd never known their granddaughter, and Hope had never met them. They'd died in a boating accident on Canyon Lake when Hope had been three. Any hope of reconciliation had gone with their passing.

Working at the Salty Dog Saloon, she'd met her share of military men. They had hit on her, propositioned her and asked her out. She'd effectively ignored their advances and refused to go out with them. She could possibly have married one and had a little help raising her daughter. But she'd refused to get into a relationship based on financial need. If she married—and that was a big *if*—it would be for love. If there really was such a thing.

Her gaze swept over John. Did he believe in love? Collette shook her head. Why even think about it? Love was not an option. Not until she had her RN licensure.

"If you think your trailer is small…" John said as he climbed the steps and ducked through the door into his camper, "you'll think it's spacious compared to this."

She followed him up the stairs, holding onto the dishtowel.

Once inside, she laughed. "You weren't kidding."

He disappeared into a miniscule bathroom and came back out with a small red and white first aid kit, setting it on the counter that doubled as a sink and a stove top. He pulled out alcohol pads and a bandage. In seconds, he'd cleaned her wound and applied the bandage. He stood back with a smile. "All better?"

She nodded. "Much better."

He turned to the microwave, punched some numbers onto the control pad and hit start. The inside lit up, displaying two fat baking potatoes. "I was waiting to cook these until the grill was almost ready."

"And then I interrupted with a spewing geyser," Collette said.

"It worked out. The coals should be hot and ready for the steaks."

"So, your meal would've been two steaks and two baked potatoes?" Collette frowned. "You sure you want to share?"

"Absolutely. I always cook extra. What I don't eat makes great leftovers." When she opened her mouth to protest, he held up a hand. "I'd rather have the company than the leftovers. Our dinner will be ready in less than twenty minutes." John opened a dorm-sized refrigerator and pulled out a pan full of steaks swimming in an aromatic sauce. "I've had them marinating since this morning."

"What do you use to marinate?" Collette pressed a hand to her loudly rumbling stomach.

He circled around her with the pan. "It's a secret. But it has beer in it. If you're allergic to beer, now's a good time to tell me." He hesitated with the steaks in hand.

"Not allergic," she informed him. "Intrigued."

"Trust me," he said. "They're good. My team lets only me grill the steaks when we get together."

"That says something. Either they don't want to do the cooking, or your steaks are really that good."

"Hmm." John tipped his head to one side. "Maybe they have been feeding my ego while I've been feeding them steaks."

Collette laughed and followed him out of the camper and down the steps. "I'll let you know after dinner."

"Can you hold the pan while I stir the coals?" John asked.

"Sure." She took the pan from him, careful not to spill the contents.

He opened the lid to the small grill and, using a long metal poker, he pushed the charcoal briquets around. When they glowed a bright red, he set the poker down, grabbed a pair of tongs from a nearby hook and laid the steaks over the grill. The juices dropped down on the hot coals and sizzled, sending up a scent that made Collette's mouth water.

"I have a feeling your guys aren't just stroking your ego." Collette leaned over the cooking steaks, closed her eyes and inhaled deeply. "How long did you say it would be?"

"Less than twenty minutes."

"I'll be right back with the salad and green beans."

"Need help?" he asked.

"Despite my recent performance, I'm not always a complete disaster. I've managed to live on my own since I was seventeen without killing myself or my daughter. I think I can finish making the salad and warming the green beans."

He dipped his head. "I'll be here, minding the steaks and my big mouth."

Collette left him at the grill and hurried back to her trailer, smiling.

It really was too bad he was in the Army. She liked her big neighbor.

She wondered how long he'd be around. Based on the fact he was living in a camper, probably not long.

With a sigh, she reminded herself that she didn't have time for men, or even one man. She was on a mission to complete her training. Anything else would have to wait until after she took the exam that would license her as a registered nurse.

Until then, she had to remain celibate and focused.

As she warmed the beans and finished cutting the salad, she glanced through the window at the man at the grill.

Her resolve would be thoroughly tested by John Sanders.

CHAPTER 3

JOHN STARED at the steaks as they turned brown on the outside, his mind on the woman in the trailer next door. She lived in a tiny trailer with her daughter. Hell, she didn't even look old enough to have a teenaged daughter. And to live in a trailer park had to mean they were living in hard times. If her pantry was anything to go by, they were existing paycheck to paycheck. Was she even working? The car parked on the pad beside her trailer was old with fading paint, scratches, dents and worn tires.

What had put her in such a precarious situation that she could barely afford to live? Yet, she'd been stubbornly prideful about refusing to be considered a charity case. The fire in her green eyes had been a complete turn-on, hitting him harder than he'd ever expected. She was a stranger, and yet he was attracted to her.

All the red flags were waving in his face. Hadn't he learned from his past relationship to steer clear of women with children?

He'd been a twenty-year-old corporal, barely out of bootcamp and advanced infantry training when he'd met Linda and her little girl, Mandy. Linda had been four years older than him and had a three-year-old daughter. Six months into their relationship, he'd been head over heels for them. At least, he'd thought he was. He had bonded with little Mandy and he'd been the only father-figure Mandy had known in her young life.

Then he'd been deployed to Afghanistan. At first, Linda had kept in touch via video calls where he'd gotten to talk to her and Mandy. Then the videos had become just voice calls and happened less frequently.

Fourteen months later, when he'd gotten back, Linda and Mandy had been gone. That's when he'd promised himself that he would never fall for a woman who had children. He'd thrown himself into training, driving himself hard, both physically and mentally. A sergeant in the Delta Force had seen him busting ass on the obstacle course one weekend and had encouraged him to try out for Delta Force.

That had been thirteen years ago. He'd been a Delta ever since. However, soon, his stint in the Army would be coming to an end. In just four more years, he'd retire. He couldn't believe how quickly the time had passed. He was the old man of the team at thirty-seven. It would be time to take a desk or training job to make room for the young guys coming up. At that point, he might not be deployed as often. He might have time to live his life like normal people.

John snorted. After years of living a high-octane life, he was looking forward to a slower lifestyle. One that included sitting on a porch and watching the sun set at the end of the day. Not charging into villages in the night, searching and destroying terrorist strongholds.

He flipped the steaks and glanced across at the trailer, catching a glimpse of Collette through the small window in her kitchen. She was looking back at him. With a lift of his chin, he returned his attention to the steaks that didn't need his attention but gave him an excuse to look away from the pretty mother.

She wasn't Linda. Hope wasn't Mandy. Hope was practically an adult and would be out of the house soon, going to college or work. For a brief moment, John could picture himself sitting in a porch swing with Collette gently swaying back and forth, watching the Texas sun set on the western horizon.

As quickly as the image passed through his mind, he mentally erased it. He wasn't retired yet and deployment was still a given. He refused to hook up with someone only for her to desert him while he was tasked with a mission that took him away for months at a time. He couldn't go through that again.

He'd looked up Linda a couple years after she'd left with Mandy. She'd married an insurance salesman and had given Mandy a couple of little brothers to herd. John had watched from a distance as Mandy had gotten off the school bus. She'd grown into a beautiful girl with a permanent frown denting her brow. No longer was she the happy little girl he'd taken to the park and pushed on the swing. For all he knew, she could've been having a bad day. His heart hurt for what could have been. She could have been his little girl. Now, at thirty-seven, he doubted he'd have children. Wasn't he getting too old?

Again, his gaze went to trailer next door and the window where Collette had been a moment before. She wasn't there.

He frowned.

"Hey, you're burning the steaks." A voice said beside him.

He spun, his hand holding the tongs out like a weapon.

Collette raised her hands. "Don't shoot. I come in peace." And she laughed. "Sorry. I didn't mean to sneak up on you. You must've been lost in thought. And it couldn't have been good thoughts based on the scowl on your face." She set the items she carried on the camp table he'd set up. "Everything all right?"

He nodded, coming back to the present and the

grill. "I'm okay. How do you like your steak?"

"Medium," she said. "Smells amazing."

She lifted a couple of plates off the stack of bowls she'd brought. "Thought we could use these."

"Just in time. This steak is done." He pulled one of the steaks off the grill and laid it on a plate she held. "That one's medium rare."

She dipped her chin and balanced the plate as he laid the meat on it. "Your steak, I take it."

"Yes, ma'am. Yours will be ready in a minute." He took the empty plate from her. "Will you check on the potatoes in the microwave?"

"Will do." She carried the other steak into the camper, laid it on the counter and opened the microwave. She gave each potato a gentle squeeze, careful not to burn her fingers. They broke open slightly, letting out steam. They were done. Removing the potatoes one at a time from the microwave, she laid them on his plate and carried it out to the table.

John was just taking her steak off the grill. He carried the plate to the table, moved a potato over to her plate then waved his hand. "I'm starved. Let's eat."

Collette opened the bowls. One contained a salad, the other the green beans. She spooned beans onto his plate. "Tell me when."

"When," he said after the first spoonful.

She laughed. "I take it you're not a big fan."

"Green beans aren't my favorite."

43

"You have a favorite vegetable?" She glanced up; the smile curling her lips made him smile back.

"Not really, unless you consider beer a vegetable." He winked. "Are hops vegetables?"

"Grain," she said, shaking her head. "Seriously, you have the eating habits of a teenaged boy."

"I survive," he argued, cutting a corner of his steak and popping it into his mouth. "And you sound like my mother."

Her cheeks flushed pink. "Touché. It's a habit I've honed over the past sixteen years."

"Hope's sixteen?" he asked and took another bite of steak.

Collette nodded. "Hard to believe, but yes." She cut off a third of the steak. "There's no way I can eat this massive amount."

"Then save it for tomorrow," he said.

"But you could have it for your lunch."

He shook his head. "It's yours."

"Okay," she said. "I'm not going to argue until I've tasted it." She cut off a small bite-sized portion and popped it into her mouth. Her eyes widened, and then she closed them and moaned.

The sound made John's groin tighten. "Good?"

After she swallowed, she opened her eyes and let out a long sigh. "Better than good. The guys aren't playing to your ego. I don't remember ever having a steak so tender and tasty." She cut off another piece and popped it into her mouth.

"When was the last time you had a steak?" he asked, casually, though he really wanted to know.

She shrugged. "It's been a while." She scooped salad onto her plate and poured a small amount of dressing on it. "Are you against salad as well?"

"Actually, I love a good salad." He reached for the bowl and dumped the contents onto his plate. "And you brought my favorite...ranch dressing." He poured the dressing over the lettuce and tomatoes and dug in to prove he didn't have the appetite of a kid. And he wasn't lying. He liked salad and *fresh* green beans. He didn't have the heart to tell her it was canned green beans he didn't like. Or canned anything, for that matter. His parents had grown a lot of their own vegetables. Nothing was quite as good as fresh-picked produce.

After a couple of bites of his steak, he reached for his drink only to realize he didn't have one. John pushed to his feet. "I've been a terrible host. Would you like something to drink? I have beer and water."

She laughed. "I'd love a beer."

"Good. That's what I'm having, and I hate to drink alone."

"Like you don't like eating alone?" She winked. "I'm betting you eat and drink alone a lot, and you don't mind it at all."

"I didn't say that," he said as he climbed the steps into the camper and reappeared moments later, carrying two bottles of beer.

Collette sat with her lips pressed together. "Why did you ask me to have dinner with you?"

"I told you. I wanted the company." He set one of the bottles on the table, twisted off the top of the other and handed it to her. "Okay, so I do like eating alone if the choice is eating alone or eating with my team. We get a lot of time together. It's nice to have some peace and quiet at times, especially after a deployment where we live together twenty-four-seven. But then it's nice to share a meal with someone else besides a bunch of guys who grunt, fart and belch at the table."

She laughed out loud and held up her hand. "I promise not to grunt, fart or belch. At least not where you can hear it."

He grinned. "Thank you. And you're a whole lot prettier than those guys. That helps."

Her cheeks turned a soft shade of pink. "You don't have to say that."

"No, I don't. But it's true." He frowned. "You have to hear that a lot."

She nodded. "Only from a bunch of drunk off-duty soldiers at the saloon where I work part time. It's hard to take them seriously."

"Sounds like the bar we hang out at." John frowned. "Salty Dog?"

She nodded. "Now, you know my entire life. I have a teenaged daughter, and I wait tables at the Salty Dog."

His frown deepened. "I don't recall seeing you there."

She looked away. "I only work on Friday and Saturday nights."

"I've been there on Friday and Saturday nights." His eyes narrowed. "But we've been deployed a bit lately."

"That must be it. I've been working there the past six months. It's the only place I can work part time and make enough in two days to keep up with the rent, food and gas."

"What do you do the rest of the week?"

"Study like crazy and take tests." She smiled. "I'm in nursing school. I gave up a fulltime job, a decent apartment and steak to go back to school."

"That's brave," he said. "How's Hope with the changes?"

Her smile softened. "She's amazing. We've never had a lot but getting my nursing license will allow me to make more money. I want to be able to help her more when she goes to college in two years. She said she'd even get a job to help out." Collette grimaced. "Problem with that is that we only have the one vehicle, and I need it to get to school and work. I have another year and a half to complete. Doesn't sound like much, but to a teenager, it's a lifetime. She's given up so much. I imagine it's not easy saying she lives in trailer park."

"There's no shame to living in a trailer park," John said. "I'm here. I don't consider it beneath me."

"We're lucky. For the most part, the residents are good people. I was careful to make sure of that. My daughter is alone when I'm at school or work. I don't like it, but we don't have much choice. She spends some time studying at our church. It's on the way home from her school. We're not far from the church or the school. Hope can ride her bicycle to school, stop and study at the library or the church and stay there until I get out of school. Then she rides home so that we get here at the same time."

John didn't like the idea of the sixteen-year-old riding her bike alone. Drivers could be careless, and any young woman alone was a target for sexual predators. He didn't voice that aloud. Collette had enough to worry about. "Where's Hope's father, if you don't mind my asking?"

Collette's lips pressed together. "I was still in high school when I got pregnant. He had just graduated and headed off to join the Army without telling me. When I notified him that I was pregnant...crickets. He didn't respond. His friends said he knew but chose to ignore me."

"Bastard," John said. "You could've sued him for child support."

"I figured if he didn't want to acknowledge his daughter, he didn't deserve any kind of visitation. I'd made the mistake of trusting him with protection.

Apparently, the protection he'd provided was faulty. I wasn't on the pill. My parents thought the only birth control a teenager needed was abstinence." She snorted. "I should've listened to them. They thought so, too."

"What about your parents? Couldn't they help you while you go to school?"

She shook her head. "They kicked me out shortly after Hope was born, wanting me to learn my lesson. I finished high school by taking the GED and went right to work. I barely made enough to pay the daycare to watch my baby and buy diapers and formula. And then they died when Hope was three and didn't leave me anything in their will." She held up a hand. "Don't go pitying me. Hope and I have had a good life. We chose to take a step down to get me through nursing school. It's the only way I'll be able to help her through college."

"Can't she get grants or loans?" John asked.

Collette nodded. "Yes, but I don't want her to have a lot of debt when she graduates. It's hard enough starting out in life without adding debt to your plate. I've been very careful not to use credit cards to get by. It's tempting, but it's also a slippery slope I don't want to slide down."

John knew he was pushing, but he couldn't help it after seeing her bare shelves. "What about food assistance?"

Collette lifted her chin. "We're not there yet. I

pick up extra shifts at the Salty Dog when we're running low on funds." She stood. "I'd rather not talk about money." She tipped her head toward the sky. "I'd rather enjoy the sunset."

John took the hint. Collette had effectively shut him down. He pushed to his feet and carried their folding chairs to the end of the camper where they had a better view of the sunset through the live oak trees.

For a moment, Collette hesitated. "I should go in and crack my books."

"Don't let me keep you if you have a test tomorrow," he insisted.

She gave a soft smile. "I'm lucky. No test until next Monday. I can afford to sit for a few minutes and breathe. I stayed a little after class to read through the next chapter, so I'm set for tomorrow's lecture." She eased into the chair and leaned back, staring out at the setting sun. "Wow. It seems like forever since I've watched the sunset like this. Most of the time, I'm driving home with the sun in my eyes, inside studying or just getting to work at the Salty Dog at this time of day."

The puffy white clouds had morphed into different shades of pink, purple and blue as the orange orb dipped below the horizon and dusk settled over Killeen, Texas.

"You know all about me..." Collette spoke softly. "What about you? What do you do in the Army?"

He hesitated for only a moment. "I'm part of Special Forces."

She glanced his way, her eyes widening. "Like Delta Force?"

He nodded. "Not like. We are Deltas." John sipped his beer and stared out as the light faded from the sky.

"The guys I've met at the Salty Dog who are Deltas aren't around much."

"That's us," he said. "We deploy more than we stay home."

"That doesn't lend itself to a stable family life."

"No, it doesn't."

"I take it you're not married." She chuckled. "Guess that should've been my first question."

"I'm not." He glanced over at her, trying to read into her expression. The diminishing light made that difficult.

Her smile was easy to see when her teeth flashed white in the dusk. "I guess if I were interested in a relationship, I would've found a way to ask that."

Her words gave him a shock of disappointment. "You're not interested in a relationship?"

She shook her head. "Not now. I have to remain focused. It's hard going back to school when you've been out as long as I have. I had to quit high school when I was seventeen and finish by GED before Hope was born. That was a little more than sixteen years ago. I've forgotten so much about math and science. I had to take online courses to get some prerequisites out of the way before they would accept me into the program. Let me tell you…it was hard. I never was very good at math. I had to study my as—Well, you get the idea." She grinned. "I have to study hard to get the grades I want. Nothing comes easy. That's why I'm going to school fulltime and working parttime. I have just enough savings to help out with the rent until I get through this."

"I'm impressed," John said. And he was. "Your determination is to be admired."

"Admire it when I'm successfully finished," she said. "I'm not going to pat myself on the back until I've passed the final licensure exam."

"Have you always wanted to be a nurse?" John asked.

"No. But having a child made me more aware of my choices. The nurses who helped deliver Hope were amazing and so caring. I wanted to be like them. It's just taken me a lot longer to get there while raising my daughter." She paused. "And here we are talking about me again. I heard right that you're not married and you don't have a wife stashed away somewhere?"

He chuckled. "That's right. I'm not, and I don't. Satisfied?"

"Mildly." Collette sipped her beer. "Why aren't you?"

"Why aren't I what?" He knew what she was asking, but he wanted to buy time to craft his answer.

She turned toward him, her eyes glowing in the light shining through his camper window. "Why aren't you married? You're good-looking, strong and have a sexy occupation. Why aren't you married, engaged or dating some hot babe?"

"Did you pay attention to the part about being deployed a lot?" He leaned his head toward her. "And I'm sitting next to a hot babe, now. Does that count?"

"No, because I'm not interested in dating you or anyone else. But you should be dating instead of hanging out with the mother of a teenager."

"You can't be older than I am."

"No?" She huffed. "Sometimes I feel really old."

"How old are you?" He paused. "Oh, sorry. That's a question a man should never ask."

"I don't mind. I'm thirty-six. Practically ancient to you youngsters."

"Ha!" he said. "I'm older than you. I'm thirty-seven."

"No way." She stared across at him. "I would never have guessed. You're well-preserved."

He laughed out loud. "And you could be Hope's sister, not her mother."

"Now, who's stroking whose ego?"

He tipped his beer up and downed the last bit. "Want another?"

"No, thank you," she said. "I need to keep my wits about me until Hope gets home. I never know if

Ryan's truck will break down, if they'll run off the road or hit a deer."

"Has it happened before?"

"No, but it could." She finished her beer and tipped her head back, staring up at the sky as the stars began to twinkle above. "Have you ever wondered where you'd be if you'd made different choices in life?"

"Sometimes." John leaned back and stared up at the same stars, seeing an entirely different set of memories. "I don't regret where I am today."

"Oh, neither do I. I wouldn't have had Hope if I'd made different choices when I was sixteen. I wouldn't change that for anything. But I do wonder where I'd have been if I hadn't fallen for the wrong guy when I was too young to be smart."

"And are you smarter now?"

"I like to think I am," she whispered.

"Is that why you're against getting involved?"

"I've become very practical out of necessity." She continued to stare up at the sky. "But sometimes, I want to be carefree."

"Being a single parent is a lot of responsibility. Especially if you don't have backup."

"Exactly. Hope is getting to be more and more independent. But she's not ready to fly on her own. And I'm not pushing her out of the nest anytime soon. She deserves to be a kid through high school."

"Unlike you," he said softly.

"Yeah, but that was a product of my poor choices." Collette leaned forward. "And on that note, I should go to my trailer and get ready for a full day of class tomorrow. Hope should be getting home soon."

As if on cue, a cellphone rang.

John glanced around for his. It was on the camp table where he'd left it, but it wasn't lit up.

Collette dug in the pocket of her shorts and pulled out a battered cellphone with a cracked screen and a worn case and answered the call. "Ryan, are you two heading back?"

She paused to listen, her brow furrowing in the limited light. "Are you two okay? Do I need to call an ambulance or the police?" Again, she paused to listen. "Are you somewhere safe? Did they leave?" She nodded. "I'll be there as soon as I can. Should only take me ten minutes. Go ahead and call your folks. Since I'm closer, I'll be there sooner. And call me back. I want to be sure you're still okay." She ended the call, stood up and spun toward her trailer.

"What happened?" John asked, trotting to keep up with her.

"That bastard Sly ran Ryan off the road. They're in a ditch not far from here." She ran up into her trailer, grabbed her purse and came back out, closing and locking the door behind her.

"Let's take my vehicle."

"It's my responsibility. You've already done enough for us," she said, heading for her car.

55

As she reached for the doorhandle, he covered her hand with his. "I have a truck. If Ryan's vehicle only needs to be dragged out of the ditch, I can do it with mine. Can you?"

She shook her head. "We'll take yours."

John cupped her elbow and led her toward his truck, helped her into the passenger seat and hurried around to the driver's side. "Where are they?"

She gave him the directions and sat back, staring out at the road ahead as he pulled out of the trailer park. Collette sat stiff and tense. And she had every right to be. The woman loved her daughter and would do anything for her.

John admired her for her strength, determination and desire to be independent. But he was glad she wasn't so stubborn that she wouldn't let him help. She needed more help than he bet she'd be willing to accept. As long as he lived beside her, he'd do what he could. He'd just have to be careful not to get too involved. She'd said she wasn't in the market for a relationship. Well, he wasn't either. Not as long as he was a Delta Force Operator. But they could be friends—only some of his thoughts revolving around Collette weren't thoughts a friend should be having. He'd have to rein those in, or he'd find himself in too deep, too quickly. Collette was a woman he could see himself watching more sunsets with for a very long time. He found that both disturbing and oddly comforting.

CHAPTER 4

COLLETTE SAT FORWARD in the passenger seat of John's truck, her heart in her throat as she scanned the ditches, searching for Ryan's truck and her daughter. "I should've known it wasn't safe for them to go out. Especially after Sly's threats. I shouldn't have let them go."

"You can't beat yourself up." John reached for her hand and squeezed it gently before returning his to the steering wheel. "You couldn't have known Sly would run them off the road."

Collette had liked the feel of his strong fingers holding hers. Too much. She wanted him to hold her hand again and make everything right. But hadn't she fought all these years to remain independent? Letting someone else shoulder her burden wasn't something she could allow to happen. This was her life and her daughter they were dealing with.

Still, she didn't own a truck and couldn't pull anything out of a ditch with her car. Nor could she afford to hire a tow truck. Relying on John to assist was the smart thing to do without setting her back a week's worth of tip money. He was shaping up to be a friend. Collette had so few friends. The only other friends she had were the people she worked with at the Salty Dog Saloon. Jim Walker, known to most as Sarge, had given her the waitress job, with the understanding she was limited on what days she could work. Sophia Phillips, or "Red" was a bartender, who'd bonded with her over their hair color. Plus, Red made sure the guys at the bar didn't harass her too much. When they got out of line, she came to Collette's defense.

Red had recently fallen for one of the Deltas. Collette turned to John. "You know Sophia, the bartender at the Salty Dog, right?"

John shot a glance her way before returning his attention to the road and the ditches. "Yes, why?"

"She's seeing a Delta."

"She sure is. She's with Blade. He's one of the members of my team. They hit it off on a trip she'd won to Cancun, Mexico."

"That's right. So, you're a member of Blade's team? I should've seen you at the saloon."

John scratched his head. "That's what I was thinking."

"I did miss a few nights when Hope got sick with

the flu. The girls covered for me and let me take a couple weeknights to make up my time."

"And we have been gone off and on lately for different assignments," John said. "I'd know if I'd seen you there; I would have remembered you."

The headlights bounced off a metal object in the ditch on the other side of the road.

"There!" Collette pointed to Ryan's truck, buried up to the axel in mud from a recent rain. She craned her neck to catch a glimpse of Hope and Ryan.

Ryan dropped down out of the truck and hurried to the passenger side to help Hope down.

John turned the truck around and parked on the shoulder, far enough off the highway to avoid getting hit. Even before he shifted into park, Collette had opened her door and was getting out.

She rushed toward the kids, crushing Hope in her arms. "Oh, sweetheart, I'm glad you're not hurt."

"I'm sorry, Ms. McCallick," Ryan said. "I tried to keep it on the road, but they rammed me several times."

Hope pushed her mother to arm's length. "I'm okay, Mom. You should've seen Ryan. He was amazing." She slipped her arm around her boyfriend. "I don't know how he didn't lose it. I was for sure we'd roll once we went down in the ditch. But Ryan handled it beautifully."

Collette's stomach roiled at the thought of the teen's truck rolling over in a ditch.

"Don't worry, we were wearing our seatbelts," Hope said. "Even if we had rolled, we wouldn't have been thrown from the vehicle."

"Don't worry?" Collette laughed, the sound more of a sob. "You were almost killed. Was it Sly?" Collette had her cellphone out, ready to call the police, the sheriff and the National Guard.

"We're not sure."

"The police should be here any minute," Ryan said.

John gave a brief nod. "Good. You'll need to tell them everything you remember, like a description of the vehicle, color, make, model, if you can remember."

"It was an older model four-door car," Hope said. "Like one of those boats some of the old people drive from back in the nineteen-hundreds."

"It was black," Ryan added. "It must've had heavily tinted windows. We couldn't see into it." He shuddered. "They just kept ramming into us. Over and over."

Hope touched Ryan's arm. "You did good. You held the road as long as you could. And when we went off, you still had control. If the ditch hadn't been muddy, we could've pulled right out." She grinned. "You were like a stunt man, rolling with the punches."

Ryan drew in a deep breath and let it out. "I did

what I had to. And, believe me, I don't want to do it again."

Sirens sounded and flashing lights strobed in the distance, moving toward them. Moments later, a Killeen police car pulled up behind John's truck, and the officer got out. Moments later, Ryan's parents arrived and hugged their son, glad he hadn't been hurt.

After Ryan and Hope explained what had happened, the police officer radioed into dispatch for the other units to be on the lookout for a large, black, older model sedan with damage to its right side. He took pictures of the damage to Ryan's vehicle, noting the dark paint that had scraped off onto Ryan's white pickup.

When he'd gotten enough information to file his report, the officer helped John and Ryan attach straps to Ryan's and John's trucks.

With Ryan at the wheel of his truck and John driving his, they pulled the stranded vehicle out of the ditch and back up onto the pavement.

Once they'd removed the straps and checked out the drivability of Ryan's truck, Ryan's parents, John and Collette followed him. Maybe it was overkill for all of them to follow, but after what had happened, Collette was glad to see the boy home.

Once Ryan was safely in his house, Hope climbed into the back seat of John's truck. John helped

Collette up into the passenger seat and rounded the front of the truck.

Collette turned to Hope. "Are you okay?"

Hope nodded, rubbing a hand across her chest. "I'm a little bruised from the shoulder strap of the seatbelt, but I'm fine."

Anger burned through Collette all over again. "When I find out who did this…I'll…I'll…"

"What, Mom?" Hope shook her head. "You have to let the police handle this," her daughter said with the voice of reason and maturity.

"You could've been killed." Collette reached for her daughter's hand and squeezed it tightly.

"But we weren't," Hope assured her.

John slipped into the driver's seat and pulled out of the Alston's driveway, heading back to the trailer park. "Everyone okay?"

"I am," Hope said, her lips twisting. "I'm not so sure Mom is."

Tears welled in Collette's eyes. She released her daughter's hand and wiped away a stray tear running down her cheek. "I was so worried," she admitted. "I shouldn't have let you go out. Not after Sly's threats."

"I know you were worried," Hope said, "but you can't protect me from everything."

"I can't lose you," Collette whispered.

"I know. I'm all you have." Hope reached for Collette's hand again. "And you're all I have. We're in this life together. I promise to be careful and aware at all times."

"I think you shouldn't ride around with Ryan for a while." Collette's lips pressed together as she watched her daughter's brow furrow.

Hope frowned and released her mother's hand. "But, Mom, Ryan's my boyfriend."

"And he and his brother are the targets of a gang. They know his truck, have attacked him once and will do it again, until they get what they want."

"They'll never get what they want if Mark flushed their drugs down the drain," Hope said. "I don't know why they're bothering Ryan, unless they're trying to bring Mark out in the open."

"That's probably what they're trying to do," John said. "If Ryan's brother has disappeared, they'll go after someone he cares about. Your mother has a point. You're in danger if you're with Ryan."

"I'm not asking you to stay away from Ryan forever," Collette said. "Just until this blows over."

"No," Hope said. "I can't abandon him. He needs me now more than ever. He wouldn't abandon me if the situation were reversed."

Collette recognized the stubborn look on her daughter's face. It was the mirror image of her own when she fought for what was right. She sighed. "Okay, but promise me you won't go out after dark until they quit harassing you two."

Hope nodded. "I can promise that. I have no

desire to be out after dark. Not if random cars are forcing us off the road." She smiled. "John, thanks for helping pull Ryan's truck out of the ditch."

"It didn't appear to have any mechanical damage," John said. "Just cosmetic. He was able to pull the fender away from the tire enough that it wouldn't rub."

Hope sighed. "He took such good care of that truck. And his parents only had liability insurance on it. It's not going to be repaired."

"You're alive," Collette reminded her.

"I know. And I'm glad for that." Hope stared through the front window. "There was a moment or two I thought things weren't going to end up so well." She grinned. "But they did...besides Ryan's truck being smashed."

"I'm worried," Collette twisted around in her seat to look at her daughter. "I can't be home all the time to keep a watchful eye on you."

"You don't have to," Hope said. "I can take care of myself. I have this down to a science. When you're not home, I'll go from school to the library. When the library is closed on Monday, I'll go to the church and study there until you get out of school. It works. You don't have to worry."

"I get home around four-thirty most days that I'm not out on the range training," John offered. "I could go by and pick up Hope at the church or school. I could let her know when I'm off."

"Despite today, you're not responsible for our family," Collette said. "We can't keep relying on you."

"Why not? I wouldn't offer if I wasn't willing to help out."

"Let him, Mom. That way I can get home sooner and maybe even get dinner on the table so you don't have to when you get home." Hope tipped her chin toward John. "Thanks for offering. I promise I'm not a whole lot of trouble."

"I'm sure you're not," John said. "Not if you're anything like your mother."

Collette snorted and held up her bandaged finger. "She's not like me. Hope is a lot more coordinated than her mother."

Hope reached for Collette's hand, a frown denting her brow. "What happened to your finger?"

"Just a little cut while chopping up a salad." Collette pulled her hand free of her daughter's grip. "I'm fine. John treated it like a professional, and I didn't need stitches."

"I can't leave you alone for a moment," Hope said.

"I wasn't alone," Collette said before she thought better.

"She was with me." John smiled at Collette. "Determined to make me eat some ruffage."

Hope laughed. "That's Mom for you. She's always trying to get me to eat healthy stuff." She wrinkled her nose. "Not a big fan."

"Same," John said. "But the salad was good, once we washed the blood off it."

Collette swung a hand at John, smacking him lightly on this shoulder. "I didn't bleed on the lettuce."

"No, you didn't. But you could have." He winked.

By the time they pulled into the trailer park, they were all smiling. Even Collette. What could've turned out to be a really bad day with Sly's threats, cutting her hand and Hope ending up in a ditch, had ended on a happier, playful note.

Admittedly, that had a lot to do with their new neighbor, John Sanders.

Collette could get used to having him around— and he was enough of a gentleman and friend to help her keep an eye on her daughter when she couldn't be there.

Granted, they'd gotten along just fine before John had moved in. They'd be fine when he moved out. However, while he was there, they'd have a little more help. The weight of her responsibilities seemed just a little bit lighter for the first time in years.

Sadly, she had to remind herself, *Don't get used to it. He won't be around forever*

JOHN PARKED his truck in front of Collette's trailer and walked the ladies to the door. After he was sure no one was inside waiting to pounce on them, he remained there until they closed the door before he backed out of their drive and pulled into the one next to theirs. His little camp trailer had the light on in the kitchen and Collette's leftover steak on the counter. He quickly slid it into a plastic bag. He could give it to her in the morning, but he might miss her. The team met early for PT. She might not be up by then. He'd be better off getting it to her before she went to bed. That way she'd have something for lunch the next day.

He worried about her. As much as she wanted him to eat healthy, he doubted she got enough to eat. She was slim enough, not too slim, but if she lost any weight at all, she'd be too skinny.

No, he had to get that steak to her that night.

He left his camper and walked around the trailer to the front door, where he knocked lightly. If they didn't answer, he'd go away and deliver the steak in the morning.

"Who's there?" a soft voice called out.

"John," he answered.

The door opened a crack, and Collette peeked out. "Hey," she whispered.

"Hey." He stood for a moment staring up at her auburn hair and green eyes in the light streaming through from her living room.

Her lips curled upward on the corners. "Did you need something?"

"No…Yes…" he stammered, and then held out the

plastic bag with the steak. "I thought you might want this for lunch tomorrow."

She smiled down at him, looked over her shoulder then stepped out onto the porch. She wore a light robe that only came down to mid-thigh. Her legs were bare, and she had a brush in her hand. She took the steak from his hand. "Thank you. I'd forgotten all about it. I would've hated for it to have gone to waste. Your steaks are phenomenal." She waited for a moment.

John didn't have anything else to say, but he couldn't make himself leave. After a long, awkward silence, he cleared his throat. "Well, I guess I'd better go."

"Yes," she agreed. Still the door remained open and neither one of them made a move.

"I'm glad Hope is all right," John said.

Collette nodded. "Me, too."

"Goodnight, Collette." John turned to leave. He was already down two steps when a voice sounded behind him.

"John."

He stopped and turned on the step where he stood.

Collette set the bag with the steak down on a table near the door. "Wait." She left the trailer, pulling the door almost closed behind her. She stood on the landing, on eye-level with him as he stood two steps down. "I wanted to thank you."

"For what?" he asked, his gaze drinking the sparkle in her eyes, reflecting the light over her door, and the way her mouth curved into a sweet smile as she stood in front of him. He had the sudden urge to pull her into his arms and kiss her.

It took all his control to keep from doing it.

"Thank you for being there for Hope when Sly was here earlier today. And thank you for feeding me the best steak I've ever had. And thank you for pulling Ryan out of the ditch." Collette leaned forward and pressed her lips to his.

His control snapped, and his arms came up around her, pulling her body against his. He crushed her lips with his.

When she opened to him, he swept in, claiming her tongue with his in a long, sensuous caress.

Her arms circled his neck, and she pressed her breasts to his chest, wrapping her calf around the back of his thigh.

The kiss went on, his hand sliding lower to cup her ass.

Collette's calf tightened around his thigh to the point her sex rubbed against the denim covering his leg.

Heat rushed through John's body, coiling low and swelling his cock, which was constricted by his jeans.

Holding her wasn't enough. He wanted to strip her naked and make love to her beneath the stars.

This woman he'd only met that day, whose path

he could've crossed at the Salty Dog but had missed by days or maybe hours. Why now? He wasn't ready for more. Not while he was on active duty, subject to deploy.

And she wasn't interested either. She had a goal she needed to remain focused on to achieve. He'd be a distraction at best.

As reason returned, he pulled back and stared down into her eyes. "You're welcome." He set her away from him. "Go inside, Collette."

Her tongue slid across her swollen lips. "What if I don't want to?" she whispered.

John's hands came up to grip her hips. He was about to pull her into his arms again when a voice called out.

"Mom?"

John dropped his hands to his sides. "Goodnight, Collette."

"Goodnight, John." She backed up a step, turned and rushed into the trailer, closing the door with a firm click.

He waited until he heard the reassuring sound of the deadbolt turning before he returned to his camper and his lonely bed, his cock as hard as a two-by-four and his pulse pounding through his veins.

His head was telling him he'd made a big mistake taking the steak over to her, and even a bigger mistake by kissing her.

His heart disagreed and rejoiced in the rush of blood heating his veins.

Collette McCallick was an amazing woman he couldn't seem to get enough of. Hopefully, time would help quench his desire. In the meantime, all he had to do was keep his hands and his lips to himself.

CHAPTER 5

COLLETTE SPENT the rest of that night staring up at the ceiling of her bedroom, reliving that kiss. Her lips continued to tingle well into the wee hours of the morning. By the time she finally fell asleep, it was almost time to get up and start her day at school. As well, that night she would have to pull an extra shift to make enough money for groceries to last to the end of the week.

When her alarm went off, she groaned and hit the snooze, going back to sleep. She repeated that three times.

"Mom!" Hope's voice interrupted a particularly sexy dream in which Collette had just gotten naked with one sexy Delta. He'd been kissing his way down her body toward the juncture of her thighs when a second "Mom!" shattered her dream.

"What?" Collette struggled to wake up, blinked

her eyes open and pulled the sheet up to her chin. She let go of the sheet when she realized she wasn't naked and there wasn't a man in her bed. "Is the house on fire?"

Her daughter stood in the doorway, looping the straps of her backpack over her shoulders. "No, but you're going to be late for class if you don't get up right now."

"What time is it?" Collette turned to stare at the bright green light of her digital alarm and gasped. She threw her sheets aside, swung out of bed and hit the ground running. "Damn. I can't be late. The instructor deducts points from the final grade if you're late to her class."

"Then you need to get up when your alarm goes off," Hope said. "I'm headed to school."

"Do you need me to drop you off?" Collette asked as she threw on scrubs.

"Like you have time?" Her daughter snorted. "No. I'll ride my bike."

"I have to work a shift at the saloon tonight," Collette said she as pulled on socks and slipped her feet into her shoes. "Do you want me to pick you up from the library or the church before I go to work?"

"I can get home on my own," Hope said.

"I don't like you coming home alone."

"Well, I don't have much of a choice. You have to work. We only have one car, and I can't get a job close enough to ride my bicycle to and from."

Collette grimaced as she yanked a brush through her hair. "I'd rather you focused on your grades than on a job."

"Yeah, but we have to eat." Hope crossed the room and hugged her mother. "Take the car. Go to work, and don't worry about me. I won't come home until I know Mr. Sanders is at his camper. Will that make you feel better?"

"And how will you know when he gets home?" Collette asked.

"I have his number. He said he'd text me when he's at his place."

Collette crossed her arms over her chest, a frown forming on her brow. "And when did you coordinate all this?"

Hope held up her cellphone. "About fifteen minutes ago while you were moaning in your sleep." A grin spread across her face. "Was he as good in your dreams as he is in person?"

"Hope McCallick!" Collette snagged a pillow from the bed and launched it at her daughter.

Hope caught it and threw it back. "It must have been a really good dream. You're blushing. He is pretty hot for an old guy."

"He's not old," Collette murmured.

Hope pointed at her mother. "Ha! So, you admit he's hot."

"I'm not admitting to anything," Collette said and ran through the trailer, collecting her purse from the counter and the steak from the refrigerator.

Her daughter stood in front of the door, her fists planted on her hips. "If he wasn't so hot, why did you kiss him last night?"

Collette's cheeks burned. "You saw that?"

"Hard to miss after he knocked on the door to deliver that steak." Hope grinned. "My bedroom window is in the front of the trailer. I could see the whole thing."

"Whatever happened to personal privacy?" Collette waved her daughter aside.

Hope moved, allowing her mother to pass her and fling open the door. "We live in a trailer park. There's no such thing as personal privacy outside the walls of this structure. For that matter, anyone can hear anything going on inside as well."

Collette paused as she passed her daughter, her heart squeezing hard in her chest. "Has it been that bad?"

Hope shook her head. "No. But I'll be glad when you're done with school. You deserve to live in a better place than this. You've worked hard to provide for me, and I appreciate that. And I know it's only until you finish your training." Hope hugged her.

"You're a good sport," Collette said against her daughter's ear. Then she kissed her cheek. "Lock up before you leave. Don't stop to talk to strangers or rescue animals."

"I know. I know," Hope said and repeated their mantra, "School is our focus."

"Good girl." Collette patted Hope's cheek and dashed down the stairs to the car. After several attempts to start it, the engine turned over and chugged to life.

Collette waited a few precious seconds while Hope mounted her bicycle and rode out of the park and onto the sidewalk leading to her high school. The location of the trailer park had been another reason she'd chosen it. Hope didn't have far to go to get to school whether she walked or rode her bike. Still, she had to go through some sketchy places to get there, thus preferring to make the journey faster on the bike.

As she left the trailer, she glanced in her rearview mirror. John's camper couldn't be seen behind her place, but the man was standing in the drive, a mug in his hand, his gaze following her, and maybe, Hope as they drove and rode away.

Her body tingled with awareness and the lingering effects of the sensuous dream. Collette was glad he was living there and wished he could stay the full year and a half until she completed her training. She supposed any time was better than none at all. It would give her a little less to worry about knowing he was looking out for Hope for the short time he was there.

Now, she'd have a lot more to worry about if she

kept lusting after the man. She couldn't afford to lose focus. Not when she had so much more to go before she finished her training.

Forcing her mind onto the road ahead, she couldn't help one last glance behind as she turned onto the highway.

He stood in the same spot. Only he held his mug up as if in salute. How had he known she was watching him?

Her chest swelled, and her core heated. She regretted that she had to work that night. Sitting outside with John, watching the sun set had been the highlight of her day. Well, coming in second to the scorching kiss that had left her sleepless and horny as hell. That had been a major highlight…with all the complications she didn't need at that particular time in her life.

She sighed and tried to banish John Sanders from her mind. It would be a long day already, without mooning over the boy next door like a teenager with overactive hormones. She might have to crank up her vibrator for a little risk-free relief later that night.

With that plan in mind, she attacked the day.

A HAND WAVED in front of John's face as he sat cleaning his rifle in the armory after a morning at the range.

"Earth to Tank," Blade said.

John batted the hand away. "What?" he answered irritated that his teammate had interrupted a replay of the night before that had been rolling around in his head all night and day long. Sitting outside, watching the sunset and drinking a cold beer with Collette had made him feel all warm and satisfied. On the other hand, that kiss had left him hot, bothered and craving more than just a kiss.

Blade held up his hands. "You don't have to bite my head off. I only asked you three times if you were joining us at the Salty Dog tonight?"

"The Salty Dog?" he asked, struggling to get his head into the here and now when he'd rather be in the night before, or with Collette instead of the smelly Deltas who'd sweated out on the qualifying range, shooting rifles, handguns and machine guns. They'd even practiced their sniper skills, aiming at targets far down range.

"What's wrong with you, Tank?" Rucker, their team leader asked. "You haven't been present all day."

John set aside his cleaning tools, having rubbed every bit of carbon and dirt off the bolt, inside of the barrel and the exterior a number of times. In seconds, he had the M4A1 rifle reassembled and set aside. "I don't know. I didn't get much sleep." Which was true. He hadn't gotten more than a couple hours of sleep after he'd laid awake thinking about a redhead with lips that made him crazy with desire.

And it wasn't just her lips. Everything about her made him want her.

"Well, toughen up, buttercup. We're going to the Salty Dog tonight to celebrate Dawg and Beth's engagement."

"I don't feel much like going."

"You have to be there," Rucker said. "Attendance isn't optional; it's required."

John would rather go back to his camper and wait for Collette to come home. Then he remembered Hope had texted him early that morning. Hadn't she said her mother would be home late? Her school didn't run late but working at the saloon would. Collette must be pulling an extra shift at the Salty Dog that night. "On second thought, I look forward to being there." He grinned. "But I need to go home and change."

"No problem. We're all going home to change. None of us want to act the fool in our uniforms off post."

"That's right. We don't need to draw any more attention to us than is necessary." Suddenly, the day was looking brighter, and the fatigue John had felt a few minutes previously disappeared, replaced by anticipation. "What time are we planning on being there?"

"Around seven. We can grab something to eat and a few beers. Since it's a weeknight, we don't want anyone showing up for work tomorrow with bloodshot eyes and smelling of whiskey Thursday morning. We already have a lousy reputation with other units on post as a group of rowdy recruits."

"Just another day with the Deltas," Dawg called out from a different table in the armory.

Seven o'clock would give him enough time to make sure Hope made it home safely and cook a meal for her. If Collette was working an extra shift, she must have needed the money for food. She couldn't buy it until she received her tips. In the meantime, there wasn't much for a teenaged girl to consume.

John had deli meat and bread. He could make sandwiches and ask her to join him at his outdoor camp table, using the same excuse he'd used to convince Collette to have dinner with him.

After having Collette spend the evening with him the night before he'd had to reconsider his desire for solitude. It wasn't all it was cracked up to be. He was lonely. Sharing a quiet evening with someone else had been nice. It had been more than sharing an evening with just anyone. He'd enjoyed Collette's company.

As the day wore on, he counted the minutes before he could leave and hurry back to his camper. On his way there, he called Hope.

"I'm on my way to the camper. I'll be there in fifteen minutes."

"Thanks," Hope said. "I'm at the church. Mr. Earles, the janitor, let me hang out in one of the

Sunday school rooms to study. He's ready to go home, and I was about to pack it in and head to the trailer. Your timing works. I'll be there around the same time."

"See ya there," he said, clamping down hard on his tongue to keep from saying something banal about being careful and watching her back. Hope's mother had probably drilled those things into her head from the moment she'd been able to ride a bike without training wheels. Besides, she wasn't his daughter or his responsibility to educate on the dangers a lone woman had to face daily. But if he had a daughter, he'd have liked her to be just like Hope. The young woman was spunky, responsible and mature beyond her years.

With his foot a little heavy on the accelerator, he made it back to the trailer park in thirteen minutes instead of fifteen, having breezed through several green lights and blowing past the slow traffic. He parked his truck next to the camper and went inside to pull the lunch meat out of the refrigerator and the bread out of a cabinet.

He glanced at his watch and hurried outside in time to see Hope turning sharply into the park, her hair flying out behind her as she pedaled her way to where she and her mother lived. The teen smiled and waved as she came to a halt and dismounted. "Wow, I thought I was getting here early." She pulled off her helmet and strapped it to the handlebars. Then she worked the combination on the cable lock looped around the base of her seat. In moments, she had the lock disengaged and the cable wrapped around the rear tire and one of the metal beams the trailer had been built on. "Did you have to wait long?" she asked as she straightened and shifted the backpack on her shoulders.

"Not at all. I was just about to make sandwiches. I have ham, turkey, chicken or roast beef. Name your poison and condiments, and I'll have it made in seconds."

Her lips pressed together, and her eyes narrowed. "I don't know. Mom likes me to go straight into the trailer and lock the door."

"I'm here to look out for you for the next hour. But if it makes you feel better, call your mother. It's just sandwiches, nothing fancy like steak."

"I heard the steak was to die for," Hope said as she dug her cellphone out of her pocket and dialed her mother's number. As she waited for an answer, her stomach rumbled. She pressed a hand to her belly and grimaced. "I guess I am hungry and I think there's only a can of chicken noodle soup in the cabinet." She focused on the cellphone. "Hey, Mom. I made it home. Mr. Sanders was waiting to make sure I was safe, so you can stop worrying. Oh, and he said he has the fixings for sandwiches. Is it okay for me to sit outside with him for a few minutes to eat?" She nodded. "Okay. I will. Love you, too." She ended the call and smiled across at John. "I can. But I need to drop my backpack in the trailer. I'll be right back."

"No hurry," he said. "It'll take a few minutes to make the sandwiches. What do you want on yours?"

"Ham, cheese and mayo," Hope said. "Thanks. I'll be right back." She dashed around the corner to the trailer. A moment later, she appeared in the window to the kitchen and waved.

John chuckled at the kid's energy and enthusiasm. He could use an infusion of that stuff. Being the old man on the team meant he had to work harder to stay in shape. It didn't come as naturally as it had when he'd been in his twenties. Still, he loved being a Delta and wouldn't quit before his time was up.

He entered his camper, laid out paper plates and assembled two sandwiches. One like Hope had requested, the other with a combination of roast beef, turkey, lettuce, tomato and mustard. He wondered what Collette liked on hers. She'd probably prefer a deli sandwich as opposed to a greasy hamburger and French fries. Quickly, John made a third sandwich with a slice of every kind of meat and both mustard and mayo on it. He filled it with lettuce and wrapped it in cellophane. He packed a slice of the tomato in a separate plastic wrapping in case she wanted it on the sandwich. He didn't want to put it directly on the sandwich because the bread would get soggy with tomato juices. If Collette didn't eat it, she could share it with a friend at the Salty Dog.

He placed it in the fridge, grabbed a couple cans of root beer, stacked the paper plates with the sandwiches one on top of the other, grabbed a couple of bags of chips and headed outside. He deposited the items on the table and glanced up at the sound of footsteps in the gravel.

Hope was just rounding the corner of the trailer. She'd changed from her school clothes into shorts, a T-shirt and flipflops and had pulled her hair up into a loose ponytail. She looked even younger than her sixteen years.

John moved the chairs from where he and Collette had watched the sunset back to the table. He held Hope's chair until she sat then claimed the one across from her.

"Thank you for feeding me," Hope said. "I would be sipping chicken noodle soup if you hadn't come along." She took a bite of the sandwich and nodded. After she swallowed, she said, "Much better than soup."

They ate in silence for a few minutes, John finishing his sandwich well before Hope. He munched on chips and drank his root beer while Hope took smaller bites and chewed slowly.

"How's school?" he asked.

She shrugged. "It's school. Full of cliques, bullies, nerds and mean girls. You know…the usual. I'll be so glad to graduate and move on." Hope took another bite of her sandwich.

"Do you know what you want to study in college?" he asked.

After she swallowed, she looked up. "I'm actually pretty good at math, and I'm interested in making money. I want to be self-sufficient and independent. Plus, I want to make enough to help my mother." She smiled. "She's always been there for me, sacrificing her needs for mine. I want to be able to give back. I never want to be in her position of living paycheck to paycheck."

"How do you feel about living in a trailer?"

Again, the teen shrugged. "I was the one who suggested it. She was going to try to work fulltime at night and go to school during the day. I knew she wouldn't have enough time to study, and she'd be exhausted all the time. I worked out a budget and found the trailer for rent with all the utilities paid. She liked that it was close enough to my school I could ride my bike or take the bus, and she could take the car to school and work. It took some convincing, but she finally saw it made sense." Hope smiled. "I was so proud of her when she turned in her resignation. She'll make a wonderful nurse and be able to afford a better lifestyle. I can't wait until she can trade in the old clunker and get a new car."

"You sound like you have it all planned out," John said.

Hope laid her sandwich on her plate. "We will succeed. First, my mother, and then I will. McCallicks are strong women. We won't settle for less." She tipped her head toward the trailer. "This is temporary. Eventually, we'll purchase our own home and have a pantry and refrigerator full of food."

John nodded. "You don't have to convince me. I believe you one hundred percent."

For a moment her eyes narrowed. "Good. Then you'll understand when I say this... Don't derail my mother. She's had a hard enough life without having a man jerk her around."

He held up his hand. "I have no intention of jerking your mother around. She deserves better."

"Damn right, she does." Hope picked up her sandwich and hesitated before taking another bite. "You might remember that before you kiss her again."

John wanted to bust out laughing but, based on the cant of Hope's eyebrows and the firm set of her jaw, she wouldn't think she'd said anything funny. "You saw that, I guess?"

She nodded and took a small bite, chewed and swallowed. "I did. I would've broken it up if she hadn't been the one to initiate it. I didn't see you setting her straight."

No, he hadn't. In fact, that had been the point at which he'd lost the control he'd been holding onto by a thread. "I admit," he said, "I find your mother attractive."

"I understand adults have physical needs," she said.

John had been in the process of taking a drink of the root beer when Hope spoke. He nearly spewed liquid all over himself and the table.

Hope's mouth quirked in half a smile. "I'm young, not stupid. My mother hasn't been on a date since… well, I've never known her to go on a date. She might be vulnerable and out of practice."

He cleared the root beer out of his throat and asked, "Out of what practice?"

"You know," she said. "Flirting, kissing and making out. Obviously, she's not a virgin, so please, if you have…relations, be well-prepared. I hear that I was the product of a faulty prophylaxis. Keep in mind that my mother is still young enough to bear children. She needs to get through nursing school before she has any more kids."

Again, he wanted to laugh at the absurdity of a grown man like himself taking advice from a girl not much more than a child. However, he knew that if he did, he'd lose all credibility with Hope. Instead, he nodded. "I'll keep that in mind. Your mother has already told me she's on a mission to get through her coursework and doesn't have time for…relations."

Hope's lips twitched. "Sometimes, things happen that aren't in your plan. You have to be ready and flexible enough to flow with it and still meet your goals."

John sat back in his chair and crossed his arms. "Are you sixteen or sixty?"

Her eyes widened. "Sixteen."

"You have the wisdom of a sixty-year-old."

"I'm a bit of a control freak. I like to plan and follow my plan. Wild cards make me nervous." She met his gaze with a steady one of her own. "Mr. Sanders, as useful as you've been, you are a wild card."

"So, I make you nervous?" He gave her a gentle smile. "I don't mean to make you nervous."

"Not so much for me, but for my mother. She needs to get her nursing license so she can help others and help herself to a better life. Until then, she doesn't need a man in her life."

"What if she married and the man provided for her."

Hope snorted. "A woman should always be able to provide for herself. If the relationship doesn't last, for whatever reason, she needs to be able to provide for herself and any children that might come along."

"Sounds like she's trained you well."

"Not at all. I learn from example. My biological father didn't help her one bit. In fact, he ignored the fact I existed altogether." She lifted her chin. "I'm glad because he's low life, bottom-dwelling pond scum."

This time John did laugh. "Don't hold back, Hope. Tell me how you really feel."

Her frown turned into a grin. "I get fired up when I think about what my mother went through when she had me. Her own parents turned her out of their home, and my sperm donor did nothing to help."

"Not all men are like him," John pointed out.

"I hope not," she said, not sounding totally convinced. "Well, at least Ryan isn't like him, and I hope you're not like him either." She pinned him with her stare. "Are you? Do you plan on being a hit and run kind of guy to my mother?"

John drew in a breath and thought hard about his answer. "I've only just met her. I don't know what, if anything, will develop. My job takes me away more days out of the year than I'm home. I have four more years until I can retire."

"So, what you're saying is you don't plan on sticking around." She laid her sandwich on her plate. "Relationships are hard. It's easier to avoid them than to work on them." The shadows in her green eyes, so much like her mother's, spoke of a deep sadness that had no business in a teenager's life.

John wanted to pull the girl into his arms and hug that look away. At the same time, he could tell she wouldn't want his pity. "It's not that I don't want a relationship; it's that I'm not good relationship material. At least, not now. It wouldn't be fair to the one I left behind for months on end."

"Is it fair for you to make that decision? Have you given love a chance? What if the person you loved loves you so much that she'd be waiting for you to return?" Hope's chin rose, and she stared at him down the length of her nose.

John looked away. "I thought I was in love once. I deployed. She was gone before I got back." With the little girl he'd grown to love as his own. "I can't do that again."

For a moment Hope stared across the table at him. She reached out to touch his hand. "It hurt, didn't it?"

He stared at the girl's hand on his. Mandy would be about her age by now. "Yes. It hurt," he said softly.

"But don't you see? Avoiding love is the coward's way of avoiding pain."

He pulled his hand from beneath hers. "Like your mother, I have to compartmentalize emotion in order to get through some days alive. I can't deploy into enemy territory thinking about the woman I left behind. I have to focus completely on my mission, without the worry of coming home to an empty house, stripped of all the furnishings and everything I ever owned."

"And my mother can't lose her focus on her studies, or she won't achieve the goal she's always wanted to attain. She has the added burden of making sure I'm fed, clothed and loved. She doesn't have time for anything else."

"I'm confused," John said. "On the one hand, you're telling me to bring protection, and on the other, you're telling me to stay away from your mother so she doesn't lose focus on her goal. Which one do you want?"

Hope sighed. "I don't know. I just know my mother hasn't looked this alive in years. And she blushed this morning. I've never seen her blush. If she needs male companionship, so be it. As long as he understands what's at stake, and she doesn't get stupid in love and throw everything away she's worked so hard for."

"I'm still not sure what you want me to do."

Hope's lips pressed together. "You're already doing it. You're relieving some of her burden by being here for me. It allows her to worry a little less. You also breathed new life into her. If that's what your kisses do for her...maybe it's what she needs. A reminder that she's still a beautiful woman."

"Oh, she is very beautiful."

"She doesn't think so. My mother only sees herself as my mother. She's got a huge heart and deserves to be loved for herself." Hope leaned toward John. "Just don't break it." With that, she leaped to her feet. "I have to do my homework now." Hope grabbed her sandwich and the root beer and turned. "Thanks for the sandwich and the chat," she shot over her shoulder as she walked away.

And like the whirlwind she was proving to be, Hope was gone.

For a long time, John sat in his chair, staring at

the empty one across from him, feeling the teenager's presence even though she wasn't there.

"I'll be damned," he muttered. The girl had put him in his place and, at the same time, had left him wondering what he should do. John prided himself in knowing exactly what he should do in any situation. Until he'd met Collette.

Kissing her had probably been the worst thing he could've done to muddy the waters. Now that he'd tasted her lips, he was like a man on drugs, craving and desperate for more. With her daughter warning him not to get her pregnant and telling him that she needed to remain focused, he wasn't sure if he should be coming or going.

His cellphone rang in his pocket. He dug it out and saw the call was from Rucker. "Tank here," he answered.

"Don't forget, we're meeting at seven o'clock. Your ass better be there." The call ended.

John had his marching orders. Even if he didn't want to, he was headed for the Salty Dog Saloon anyway. Collette would be there, and he wanted... no...*needed* to see her in spite of, or maybe because of, all her daughter had shared and warned him about.

CHAPTER 6

COLLETTE WORKED the busy after-work shift, confident in the knowledge her daughter had made it home safely, thanks to the watchful eye of her new neighbor, John.

She smiled as she took orders, cleared tables and served more drinks.

"Hey, Collette, when are you going to marry me?" a slightly inebriated customer yelled out loud.

"Never in a million years," she responded, setting his mug of beer in front of him. "Besides, you're married."

"We could move to Utah," he said. "They allow a man to have more than one wife there, don't they?" He settled a hand on her ass.

Collette slammed the tray she'd been carrying onto the table, grabbed Joe's hand and bent his thumb back until the grown man squealed like a little girl.

"Why do you have to be so mean to me?" Joe cried. "I asked you to marry me, not have my children."

She waved her free hand over her torso. "This is my body. You have no right to touch it in any way whatsoever. Got it?"

He winced, sweat breaking out on his forehead in his effort to keep from yelling out loud. "I got it. Just let go before you break my thumb."

Bending it back just a little more, she stared into his eyes. "Touch me again, and I'll *break* your thumb."

"I won't touch you," Joe said. "Promise."

Collette stared at him through narrowed eyes. "You'd better not. If you do, I'll break it…slowly." Then she let go of his hand, brushed her hands over her shirt and skirt, lifted the tray full of empty containers to her shoulder and sailed across the room.

She was tired of men thinking they could touch her any time they wanted. If Sarge got mad at her for roughing up a customer, then so be it.

As she neared the counter, Red, the pretty strawberry-blonde bartender clapped. "Way to go. I've been wanting to put Joe in his place for ages. And here you are, doing it for me. Bravo, Collette." Red turned to Sarge as he pushed through the door to the kitchen.

"What are we celebrating?" he asked. "The fact you have all the tables loaded with drinks and everyone served?"

Red snorted. "Oh, hell no. We're celebrating the fact Collette stood up to Joe and his octopus-like hands."

Sarge frowned. "Where is he? I need to cut him off and ban him from drinking alcohol while he's in my building." The owner of the bar scanned the room, his gaze coming to rest on the construction worker seated amongst a table full of his blue-collar pals. "I'm going to have a word with him." He pushed his sleeves up his arms and started for the gate that would allow him to walk through the bar counter onto the dance floor.

Collette caught his arm. "It's okay. I handled it."

"Yes, she did," Red said. "I don't think Joe will touch her again. I think he likes having an opposable thumb." She chuckled as she filled a mug full of beer from the tap. She set it on Collette's tray, along with a couple of longneck bottles of designer beer and a bowl full of pretzels. "Is this tray for him?" she asked.

Collette nodded. "It is."

"Good. I want to watch you break his thumb." She pushed the tray toward Collette.

"I'm not sure I want to see that," Sarge said. "Maybe I should deliver the drinks just this once."

Red glared at her boss. "You spoil all the fun."

"I can't have my staff injuring customers," he said.

"And you can't have your customers sexually harassing your staff," Red shot back. She crossed her arms over her chest and stared Sarge down.

His frown deepened, but he didn't take the tray and deliver it himself. "Take the tray. If he bothers you again, I want to know. I'll throw his butt out of here so fast, he won't know what hit him."

Stiffening her spine, Collette lifted the heavy tray and marched back to the table where Joe, the married man with the wandering hand, sat with a group of his friends.

"I knew you'd be back for more." Joe smiled smugly as he reached for her ass, his hand landing on her hip instead.

Collette nearly dropped the tray full of drinks.

"Leave her alone," one of his friends said. "We're here to drink, not harass the staff."

"I'm not harassing," Joe insisted. "I'm flirting. And she came back, so she must have liked it."

"I don't," Collette said, her tone flat, her jaw clenched so tightly, she was afraid she might break her teeth. "You have three seconds to get your hand off me."

Joe laughed and slid his fingers around to cup her bottom. "Aw, you're just teasing old Joe."

"Two seconds," she stated clearly.

"I'm liking what I'm feeling," he said.

"One." Collette shoved the full tray into Joe's face,

spilling beer, mugs and bottles into his lap. Glass broke as it hit the concrete floor.

Joe tipped backward in his chair and nearly fell over. When he regained his balance, he lurched to his feet. "Got a little sass going there, do you?"

She planted her fists on her hips and squared off with Joe. "There's a lot more where that came from. Do you just want me to whip your sorry ass?"

"As long as you sit on my face in the process," he said, his words slurring. "Now, come here and give me some of that sugar. I love me a feisty woman."

Feeling sorry for Joe's wife, Collette could do nothing but defend herself. If that meant breaking Joe, then she'd love the hell out of doing it.

This time when he reached for her, she was ready. His alcohol-dulled senses were no match for the few self-defense techniques she'd learned. Collette grabbed his hand and twisted around, coming up behind him. She shoved that hand up the middle of his back between his shoulder blades.

The man chuckled, and then grunted when she pushed it up further. "You're hurting me, sweetheart. Why don't you let go and give me that sugar instead?"

Tired of fooling with the man who couldn't take a hint if it hit him square in the face, she rammed his hand higher up the middle of his back. "Don't ever touch me again, Joe. Or any of the waitresses here at the Salty Dog."

"Hey, I didn't mean nothing by it," he said, his

voice getting higher. "You don't have to hurt me. I'm a paying customer." He shouted across the barroom, "Sarge, can you call off your rabid dog? She's hurting my paying arm."

Sarge crossed the floor, coming to stand in front of Joe.

"Thank goodness," Joe said. "Tell her to let go, will ya?"

Sarge exchanged glances with Collette. "I'll take it from here."

"Not until he apologizes and promises to leave us alone," Collette said between clenched teeth.

"I'm sorry already," Joe said, standing on his toes to relieve the pain. "I promise not to touch you ever again."

"He's promised that before," Red said from behind the bar.

"I mean it this time," he said. "I swear."

"He's apologized and promised." Sarge came to stand behind Joe with Collette. "I've got this, now."

Collette didn't release her hold until Sarge had a good grip on the man's arm.

"Collette, do you want to press charges on this man for sexual harassment?" Sarge asked. "Say the word, and I'll have the cops here so fast, you'd think they were on standby. And if I know Red, she's already called them."

"I said I wouldn't do it again," Joe said. "You call the cops and my wife will kill me."

"You should've thought of that before you made an ass of yourself," Sarge said, pushing Joe's wrist up higher between his shoulder blades.

"I won't press charges…this time," Collette said. "But if he ever does this again to any of us here at the Salty Dog, I will." She wasn't sure how she'd pay for a lawyer to represent her, but the man had to learn he couldn't get away with that kind of disrespect.

"You won't have to worry about him harassing you here anymore. Not here, anyway," Sarge said. "He's not welcome in the Salty Dog from now on. Do you hear that, Joe?"

"What?" Joe tried to turn around, but Sarge held firm. "You mean my money ain't good enough for your crummy bar?"

"No," Sarge said. "Your manners aren't good enough. I won't tolerate anyone harassing my wait staff. You've gotten away with too much for too long. It ends here." The retired sergeant marched the offensive man toward the front door.

"Guys!" Joe called out to his buddies at the table. "You gonna let them do this to me?"

Not one of them rose to defend him.

"I can have you up on charges of assault and battery," Joe blustered.

"I don't think you'll find one witness to vouch for you in here. But there are dozens who will testify that you harass the women," Collette said as she hurried toward the door, opening it for Sarge to push

Joe through unimpeded. "Do you want to take that to court?"

Collette followed Sarge outside into the parking lot. The sun was well on its way toward the horizon, and dusk was settling over the town. The bright orange ball hung low in the sky, blinding Collette's gaze to the west. She trained her attention on Joe as Sarge gave him a shove before releasing his wrist.

Joe stumbled forward, righted himself and turned, a sneer curling his lip up on one side. "I don't need this stinking shithole anyway. The food isn't good enough to feed to my dog, and the drinks are watered down."

Sarge crossed his arms over his chest. "Leave, Joe, or I'll have the police remove you from my property."

Now that he was free of Sarge's hold on his arm, Joe puffed out his chest and stared down at the retired Sergeant Major. "I'll go when I'm good and ready."

Sarge stepped forward, his hands clenched into fists. "You'll go now."

"Just leave, Joe." Collette stood beside Sarge. "You've caused enough trouble for the night."

"You're the one who started it," Joe said jabbing his finger at her. "If you hadn't taken offense to a little lighthearted teasing, we wouldn't be standing in the parking lot."

"How would you like it if someone grabbed your

crotch when all you wanted to do was your job?" Collette demanded.

"I didn't grab your crotch," Joe shouted. "I touched your ass like a friend would do. I thought you were my friend."

"Well, you're not. And you didn't ask my permission to touch me. I didn't like it, and I told you not to do it again. And you did it again."

Joe lunged for her.

Collette backed up so fast, she tripped over the sidewalk curb and fell on her ass.

Joe was almost on her when he was jerked backward and was thrown to the ground.

John Sanders towered over the downed man. "Get in your car and get the hell out of here. Now." His words were spoken in a quiet yet firm tone. John's brow dipped low on his forehead, and he stood with his fists bunched and his legs braced for a fight.

Collette's heart swelled as she scrambled to her feet. The man was every bit the "Tank" his friends called him. In his current mode, he was a gladiator ready to pummel his opponent into the ground.

Joe didn't stand a chance against the big guy, and he knew it. He crab-walked backward until he was out of swinging range of those big fists. "You haven't seen the last of me," Joe called out as he hurried toward his two-door, older model truck. He climbed in, started the engine and spun gravel as he gunned the accelerator, shooting him out of the parking lot and onto the street.

Red stepped up to Sarge. "I called the cops and told them the make and model of his truck. They should be here any minute."

Sirens sounded nearby as two Killeen police cars whipped into the parking lot.

"He just left." Sarge pointed to the disappearing taillights. "White, two-door truck." He gave them the license plate number and stood back as the officers sped after Joe.

Not much further down the street, Joe had stopped at a red light. The police were on him, pulling him over.

"They'll get him for driving under the influence," Red said.

"Will the courts come back against the Salty Dog Saloon?"

Sarge shook his head. "I'll testify we stopped serving him booze after his third beer." Sarge clapped his hands together and turned back to the entrance of the saloon. A crowd of customers had gathered. "Show's over. How does a drink on the house sound?" A cheer went up, and the patrons pushed through the door, eager to get their free drinks.

"I'm sorry I brought you all this trouble," Collette said to Sarge.

"No," he touched her shoulder, "I'm sorry I didn't

kick his sorry ass out sooner. But you did prove one thing…"

"And what was that?"

"You can handle a tough customer." Sarge grinned. "I didn't know you had a badass streak inside you. You sure you weren't a marine or something?"

Collette shook her head. "No, but Hope and I took self-defense lessons that were offered at the YMCA. I'm glad we did; they came in handy."

"I could stand a few of those lessons myself," Sarge said. "Come on, Red's going to have her hands full filling drink orders. I need to help her behind the bar."

"And I need to serve those drinks." Collette fell in step behind Sarge, moving slower so that John could catch up with her. "Thank you," she said.

"For what?"

"For coming to my rescue, once again."

"I didn't do much. You and Sarge had everything under control."

Collette laughed. "Hardly. Joe just couldn't see that he was doing anything wrong."

"Well hopefully, the cops will convince him."

She nodded. "Kind of leaves me feeling crappy. I don't want Sarge to lose money by losing a customer."

"He doesn't need customers like that. If he's been

harassing the staff, he needed to learn a lesson. And you ladies need to be protected."

"Anyway, thank you," she said and entered the building. Then a thought occurred to her, and she spun toward John. "Is Hope all right? Are you here to tell me something's wrong at home?"

John shook his head. "Hope's fine. I made sure she went into the trailer and locked the door. She and I ate sandwiches for dinner at my outdoor camp table."

Collette smiled. "She texted me for permission. Which I appreciated. How did dinner go?"

John tilted his head to one side. "Interesting. Hope is one smart young lady. I believe she has a future in counseling or law. She's very convincing and passionate about her beliefs."

Collet's brow wrinkled. "Oh, dear. Did she try to give you all the advice? Sometimes, I think she's the mom and I'm the kid. The girl researches psychology and politics for light reading. She knows what buttons to push and how to form an argument you can't dispute."

John chuckled. "I noticed." He followed her through the tables to the bar.

Collette collected a tray full of drinks and hefted it up onto her shoulder. "What did she say?" she was almost afraid to ask. Her daughter had an over-inflated sense of responsibility for anyone who stepped into her sphere of influence. "Did she try to advise you on how to live your life?"

"A little. Only where it concerns you," he said.

With her hands full of drinks to be delivered, Collette couldn't hang around and drill John for answers to the million and one questions she had roiling around in her mind. What had Hope talked with him about? Her daughter had a protective streak a mile wide. She mothered Collette almost as much as Collette mothered her.

When she circled back around to the bar where John had been standing. He wasn't there. Then she noticed a group of men who'd taken a table in the far corner. John was among them. She recognized Red's guy, Blade, and vaguely recalled a couple of the others.

Red joined them briefly while Sarge manned the bar. There were several women among the men, each standing with a particular man. They all looked like friends, even the women,

Collette sighed, collected empty bottles and mugs from a table and hurried to the bar.

Sarge tipped his head toward the group of Deltas. "You should go hang out with them."

"Me?"

"Yes, you," he said. "You're young. You know Tank and Red. You'd fit right in."

"I'm here to work. I don't get tips if I don't deliver what the customers want."

"Are you in a bind?" Sarge's bushy eyebrows

dipped, forming a V over his nose. "I can loan you some money to tide you over."

"Not unless you can tide me over for the next year and a half." She shook her head. "We're okay. I'm sure there will be enough money in tips to keep us going." She hoped. Her checking account was down to small change, and she'd already dipped into her savings twice that month. She had to make it last for their rent. Hope had helped her design a budget. It would only work if they followed it to the letter. Tip money was the wild card. Some days were better than others. The good days allowed them to purchase meats and fresh vegetables. Bad days, she just put the money aside and waited until her next shift to go out and buy more food.

Her gaze went to the group laughing and hugging a couple. They seemed to be congratulating them. The woman held up a ring on her left hand. Either they'd just gotten engaged or they had married.

Another sigh escaped her lips. A year and a half never seemed too long before. Why now?

Because she wanted to be with John. She wanted to know the other men on his team. The men he worked with on a daily basis. The ones who had his back in battle. The man was lucky. He had a brother-hood of friends surrounding him.

For the first time in a long time, Collette envied someone else. What would it be like to have a group of friends who had your back and would die for you, if it came right down to it? Her life with Hope was full and happy. She had no reason to envy anyone.

Yet, in the back of her mind, she knew why she was feeling that way. About the time she finished her training, Hope would be graduating high school and leaving home to go to college.

Collette would be well and truly alone.

Her gaze went to John.

He was looking her way, a slight frown puckering his brow. He mouthed the words, *Are you all right?*

She nodded, heat rising up her neck and filling her cheeks. Did the man read minds? Or was she too obvious with her emotions. She'd been told her expressions were very telling. Collette forced her face to smooth and expressionless when she next glanced toward John.

His frown had deepened. He left his friends and crossed the room to stand in front of her. "Are you all right?"

"Yes. Of course." Collette dodged around him and hurried toward an empty table littered with mugs, bottles and whiskey glasses. Without looking up, she hurried through the motions of clearing the table.

"Are you afraid of me?" John whispered.

Her head jerked up. "No. Not at all. I trust you." She laughed. "I don't know you that well, yet somehow, I trust you."

"I'd never hurt you," he assured her.

Not intentionally, maybe. Collette had a feeling

he'd hurt her eventually. Either she would be too busy to make the effort, or he'd decide to stick to his plan and remain attachment-free until he retired in four years. Collette wasn't convinced she wanted the emotional strain of the hurt that was sure to come. Not when she needed to channel all her energy into school and making passing grades. Everything she did was for her daughter.

As she studied John, she wished, just once, that she could do something for herself.

And what would she do? Or who? A thrill of excitement rippled through her as she relived the dream she'd started the day with. She'd gone a long time without making love with a strong, virile man. Battery operated boyfriends didn't count, nor were they as emotionally satisfying. Then again, they weren't emotionally draining.

She sighed and kept serving. The tips were good that night. The customers must have felt sorry for how Joe had treated her. They'd tipped heavily for a weeknight. And thank goodness. She'd be able to buy some of the groceries they needed so desperately, and she'd show John she wasn't a charity case.

During the workweek, the bar closed a few minutes after ten. Collette's feet hurt as she stacked chairs on the tables and swept the floor. Sarge followed behind her, mopping up the stickiness of spilled drinks.

By the time they were done, Collette was so tired

she could have crawled into her car and slept there. Much as the idea appealed to her exhausted body, she had a daughter at home.

The group of Deltas had left sometime after nine-forty-five. John must have left with them. She hadn't seen him since.

Collette couldn't help being a little disappointed that he hadn't at least tried to say goodbye. Then again, he wasn't her boyfriend, fiancé or spouse. She had no hold on the man and no right to be disappointed.

Yet she was.

"Go home, Collette," Red said. "We'll finish up what little is left."

"You heard her," Sarge seconded. "You can't fall asleep in class. You're supposed to be teacher's pet."

"She doesn't have pets," Collette murmured. "But since you insist, I'll go home. I'd like to see my daughter before she goes to sleep."

"See you Friday?" Sarge asked.

"I'll be here unless something big comes up." She laughed. "Who am I kidding? Nothing big comes up in my life."

"Never say never," Red warned. "Or is it never say nothing?" She shrugged and went back to work washing mugs and wine glasses. "Whatever."

Collette collected her purse from beneath the counter, found her keys and walked out of the building.

It took a few minutes for her eyes to adjust to the darkness. She stood for a moment until they did, and then set out for her car where she'd parked it under one of the bright lights. As she neared it, a shadow detached itself from the side of a pickup. She caught the movement out of the corner of her eye. Her pulse leaped and she stopped in her tracks, unsure of whether she should run back to the bar or dive into her car. She spun, ready to race back to the bar where there were others to protect her.

She moved.

The shadow moved faster.

CHAPTER 7

COLLETTE'S PULSE pounded so hard it banged against her eardrums, so loudly she couldn't hear herself think. She had to make it back to the bar before whoever it was caught up to her. She took off at a run.

Footsteps sounded behind her.

She ran faster.

"Collette," a familiar voice called out. "It's me... John."

Collette staggered to a stop, breathing hard, afraid she'd heard wrong. When she turned to face the man following her, she realized she'd been running for nothing.

John closed the distance between them, and the light shined down on his rugged face.

Collette pressed a hand over her pounding heart. "You scared me."

"Do you always walk out here alone at night?"

"No," she said, dragging in a shaky breath. "I usually wait for Red or Sarge. But they let me go early so I could get home to see Hope before she goes to sleep." She fumbled with her keys and moved toward the dilapidated car she'd been driving since she'd left home with a small baby to care for. "Why are you still here?" she asked. "I thought you'd left when your friends did."

"I was worried Joe might show up and stir up more trouble." He waited for her to open the car door and slip inside. "Do you mind if I follow you home?"

She laughed. "Why would I mind? You live next to me." Collette twisted the key in the ignition. The engine turned over slowly and died. "Not now," she whispered. She switched off the ignition then tried again. This time nothing happened. She checked the gauges, and then noticed the interior light wasn't shining down on her. "Well, crap." Collette pushed open the door and got out.

"Problem?" John asked.

"I think I have a dead battery."

"Any idea how old it is?" John asked.

"I replaced it back before Hope started high school. Maybe three or four years."

"The Texas heat can be hard on batteries. I've got jumper cables. Let's see if the battery just needs to be charged."

Collette crossed her fingers. It seemed like every time she got a little money, something big came up and she had to spend it on that, instead of food. She couldn't get around without her car. If she needed a battery, her tip money would have to go toward that. Hopefully, it just needed to be charged. Maybe she'd left a light on somewhere and had inadvertently drained the battery.

Within a few short minutes, John had his truck parked beside her car and the cables connected to each vehicle's batteries.

"Crank it," John called out from where he stood in front of her car.

She turned the key. Though sluggish, the engine turned over and the car started.

Collette heaved a sigh. At least the engine was still performing. The big question was would there be enough of a charge in the morning to start it? She couldn't be late to class. The instructor had no patience for students who were tardy or missed a day.

"You go ahead. I'll follow in case the engine dies on the way." John coiled the cables and stowed them behind the back seat in his truck.

Collette backed out of the parking space and headed home, praying the battery was charging and wouldn't be a problem in the morning. She hated that every time she turned around, John had to bail her out of trouble. She'd handled her life just fine on her own, up until now.

The headlights behind her gave her too much of a

sense of comfort. She could get used to having a backup.

With a sigh, she pulled into her parking space beside her trailer. A light shone from her daughter's bedroom window. Good. Hope was still awake. Her day was never complete until she spoke to her daughter before she went to sleep. The night she couldn't continue that ritual would come all too soon when Hope went off to college. Until then, Collette made it a priority to at least hug her only child and say goodnight.

She parked her car, afraid to turn it off.

John drove around the back of her trailer and parked his truck. He returned on foot and stood beside her vehicle when she switched off the key. "Try starting it now," he said.

Collette held her breath and turned the key. The engine started right up. She let out a relieved breath, turned it off again, got out and locked the door behind her. When she turned to John, she smiled up at him. "Once again, I find myself beholden to you. How can I repay you?"

"You don't have to. That's what friends do."

He stood close enough to her that she could raise her hand and touch his chest. Collette's hand was halfway up before she realized that was exactly what she'd been about to do. She let herself continue and laid her fingers on his chest. "Does that mean we're friends now?"

He captured her hand in his. "I'd like to think so."

She stared at where his fingers wrapped around hers. Her pulse kicked up, and butterflies erupted in her belly. "Thanks, John. Thanks for being at the saloon tonight and saving me from Joe."

John stared down into her eyes. "I heard you saved yourself from that jerk. I'm impressed."

"Yeah, well, he almost got the best of me in the end." She inhaled and let out a frustrated breath. "I need to keep up my guard."

He lifted her hand to his lips and pressed a kiss to her fingertips. "You don't have to with me."

"Thank goodness," she whispered, her breath lodging in her throat.

The light in her daughter's room blinked off, pulling Collette back to reality. She stepped back. "Goodnight, John."

He nodded, letting go of her hand. "Goodnight, Collette."

She stood before him a moment longer.

"Kiss him, already," Hope's voice called out through the thin walls of the trailer.

"You heard your daughter," John said with a smile.

"What if he doesn't want me to?" Collette asked her daughter, though her gaze connected with John's in the light from her porch.

The rickety blinds in the window beside them blinked open, and Hope's face appeared. "Trust me, he does. Now, get on with it. I want a hug before I go to sleep." The blinds closed with a snap.

Heat flooded Collette's cheeks. "Just because she said so doesn't mean we have to."

She'd barely gotten the words out when John pulled her into his arms and claimed her lips.

Collette melted against him, her body pressing against the hard plains of his, her lips opening to allow him in.

He swept past her teeth, his tongue caressing hers in a sexy dance she didn't want to end.

But end it had to.

When he finally raised his head, he pressed his lips to her forehead and straightened. "How was that?" He directed his question to the window.

"That's more like it," Hope said.

"I'd better go," Collette said, surprised at how breathy her voice was.

"Yes, you'd better."

"Sorry for the audience," she said with a grimace.

He chuckled. "Your daughter is a force to be reckoned with."

"You're telling me?" She shook her head. "With her strong will and solid moral compass, I'm convinced she's going to be all right in this world."

"I think you're right." He glanced toward the window. "Did you hear that?"

"Whatever," Hope said. "Goodnight, Mr. Sanders."

"Goodnight, Hope," he said with a laugh. "I'll be up early if you need me to jumpstart your car again."

"Thanks." Collette started to pull out her key.

"The door's unlocked," Hope said through the window.

Collette turned the knob and opened the door. With one last glance toward John, she entered the trailer, closed the door between them and leaned against it. For a moment, she gathered her wits, knowing her daughter would drill her for all the details of what was going on between her and John.

When Hope didn't emerge from her bedroom, Collette went in search of her daughter.

Hope lay on top of her comforter, making an entry in her journal.

"How was your day?" Collette asked.

"Noneventful." Hope continued to write.

"For a noneventful day, you seem to have a lot to write about." Collette didn't try to look at what her daughter wrote in her journal. If Hope wanted her to see it, she'd show her.

"I'm just writing down my thoughts. I do that sometimes. It's interesting to see how my ideas change and morph over time." She finished her sentence with a flourish and smiled up at her mother. "Mr. Sanders seems to be a nice man."

"Yes, he does," Collette agreed. "Are you going somewhere with that statement?"

Hope lifted her shoulders and let them fall. "No. It was just an observation."

"Does it bother you that we kissed?" Collette asked.

"It bothered me more that you two are obviously attracted to each other, but you just stood there looking at each other like a couple of awkward teenagers." She swung her legs over the side of the bed and stood. "I know how determined you are to succeed at your nursing program and working part time, but I want you to be happy as well."

"And you think John...Mr. Sanders can make me happy?" Collette opened her arms.

Hope stepped into her embrace and hugged her tightly. "No. I don't think he can make you anything. You're the only one who can make yourself happy."

Collette chuckled. "Sometimes, I think you have a very old soul."

"And I think you didn't have the chance to be a normal teenager when you got pregnant with me. You've had to be an adult before you should have had to. You've gone nonstop since." Hope leaned back, her arms still around Collette. "The world does not revolve around me. You have to have your own life and happiness."

"I know," Collette's eyes filled with tears. "You'll be going off to college soon and—" Collette swallowed hard.

"You'll be alone," Hope finished. "Are you ready for that?"

"I will be." Collette squared her shoulders. "You won't have to worry about me. I'll be in a nice house, doing what I love most, helping others."

"And what about love?" Hope asked. "Are you open to the possibility? You can't judge all men based on your experience with my biological father."

"I know. But it's hard to trust."

"Yes, it is. But the risk might be worth it." Hope brushed a tear from Collette's cheek. "Think about it. Sometimes, the risky things are worth taking a chance."

"You truly are an old soul."

"No, I'm just a dorky teen who thinks she knows everything when she's barely begun to live her life." Hope winked. "Don't worry, I plan on living it to the fullest."

"With Ryan?"

Hope shrugged. "Maybe. I have time to decide." She turned her mother around and gave her a gentle shove. "Now, go to bed. You have school tomorrow, and you can't be late."

"Yes, ma'am," Collette said with snappy salute. She paused in the doorway. "Are you going to the library or the church tomorrow?"

"I think I'll go to the church. I can have a room to myself with no one around."

"I can pick you up from there on my way home."

"That would be nice. Ryan's going to take me to school tomorrow, and he can drop me at church after school before he goes to work."

"Sounds like a plan. I'll be by around five to get you."

"Good," Hope slipped back into her bed and tucked her legs beneath the comforter. "They lock up at five on nights they don't have choir practice or services."

"Who locks up after you leave?"

"Either the secretaries or Mr. Earles, the janitor." Hope slipped her journal into the nightstand. "I like the secretaries. They always say hello."

"And the janitor?" Collette asked.

"I see him cleaning in the hallways a lot. He doesn't say much. Sometimes, I catch him staring through the door at me." Hope shrugged. "It's a little creepy."

"Are the secretaries close if you need them?"

Hope nodded. "Yeah. I study in one of the Sunday school rooms near their offices."

"Good. Be sure they know you're there in case anything happens."

Hope snorted. "Like anything would ever happen at the church."

"You never know what Sly will try. If he was responsible for running Ryan off the road, he might make you a target to get Ryan to pressure his brother."

"Ryan hasn't had any more run-ins with Sly since being rammed off the road." Hope laid back on her pillow. "Maybe he finally realized he's picking on the wrong guy. If Sly has a gripe, he needs to take it up with Mark."

"Isn't that the issue, though?" Collette asked.

Hope nodded. "No one can find Mark. Ryan's parents are frantic. They've looked everywhere they can think of, and there's no sign of him. It's as if he's fallen off the face of the earth."

Collette worried that Mark might be lying somewhere in a shallow grave, but she didn't say that to Hope.

"Why don't you go to the library tomorrow? There are more people there."

Hope's lips pressed together. "That's the problem. There are more people, including small children, who don't understand what quiet means. I'll go to the church where I'll get my heavenly silence. Seriously, I have a biology test to study for. I need to think."

"Okay. I'll pick you up there."

"Goodnight, Mom." Hope leaned over and switched off the lamp on her nightstand. "I love you."

"I love you more," Collette said.

Hope yawned and closed her eyes. "I love you mostest."

Collette pulled the door closed and got ready for bed. After showering, she slipped into a short night-gown and padded barefooted into her small room.

She found herself looking at the space from a different perspective.

What would it be like with John in this small space? His head would be really close to the ceiling and his shoulders would span the room. Heck, he'd fill her double bed with his long length, leaving his feet dangling over the end.

The trailer wasn't built for tall, muscular men. It was barely big enough for her and Hope.

She peeked through the blinds out the back side of the trailer to the smaller camper where John lived. Though her home was small, his was even smaller. How did a man as big as John live for any length of time in such a confined area?

If she were a good friend, she'd invite him to share her larger space. Hell, Hope had more or less given her permission to pursue the man. She'd condoned their kissing to the point she'd told them to get on with it.

Collette laughed. Whatever man Hope fell in love with would have his hands full. Her daughter was definitely a force to be reckoned with. She made her mama proud. Hope wouldn't be foolish enough to get pregnant at sixteen. Collette had to admit, she'd found herself holding her breath through the year. She'd feel better when Hope turned seventeen without surprising her with a grandchild.

Unlike her own parents, Collette wouldn't turn out her own daughter to make it on her own. She'd help her get the education she'd need to support a child and make a comfortable home for them.

With her heart a little lighter and her lips still tingling from her second kiss with John, Collette slid between the sheets, her skin super sensitive after dreaming she'd been naked with the Delta.

Now that she had Hope's blessing to do what made her happy, Collette wondered if she could have a fling with John and come out unscathed at the end.

He'd clearly said he wasn't relationship material, what with his job and deployments. He might be open to it in four years when he retired from the Army. Could she wait that long? It made more sense to wait. After all, she'd told him she wasn't interested in relationships until she'd finished nursing school.

Waiting was the right answer.

Her core heated with the remembrance of her dream.

Waiting was the right answer. Would she last four years? She didn't think she'd even make it through the self-imposed year and a half it would take to get her nursing licensure.

Her body was on fire with pure, physical need only a flesh and blood man could satisfy. And not just any man.

John.

CHAPTER 8

JOHN WAS UP EARLY the next day after lying awake for another night, his body aching with need. He wasn't sure how much longer he'd be able to see Collette before his control snapped and he carried her off to his bed to make mad passionate love to her.

What he needed was a mission to carry him off to the far side of the world to give him a chance to cool off. The time away would give her a chance to finish her schooling. By then, she might not be interested in him at all.

Such was the nature of a Delta Force operator's life.

Then why the hell wasn't there a mission for them? When he wanted one, it wasn't forthcoming. When they didn't want to deploy, they could be guaranteed the nastiest, most dangerous situation would come along, and they'd be called up to handle it.

He sighed as he dressed in his uniform, made a cup of coffee and glanced out his window toward Collette's home a few feet away from his. She could be getting a shower, standing naked beneath the spray. He could throw his coffee cup that far very easily. And yet she might as well be on the other side of town. She wasn't interested in a relationship. Collette had been adamant about that.

Then why had she kissed him? Not once but twice.

And it hadn't been a sweet, friendly kiss to say thank you. It had been the full-on, toe-curling, pulse-racing kind that set his blood on fire and made his cock hard enough to drive nails.

Yeah, he was in a bad way he couldn't take care of on his own. He needed her like he needed to breathe.

All night long, he'd gone through different scenarios in his head, and he'd come to the same conclusion with all of them.

Collette wasn't the kind of woman who could be happy with a fling. She was the all or nothing kind. If she couldn't have it all, including a picket fence she'd half-paid for, she would abstain altogether.

Hell, she deserved more than a fling. After being ditched by her baby daddy and thrown out of her parent's home, she didn't need another man to muck up her life. She needed one who would stick around and make her life easier, not harder.

By the time he'd left his bed, John was clear about what he had to do.

He had to stay away from Collette and her daughter. For his peace of mind and to keep from hurting her when he had to leave. Better to break it off before it even got started.

Two kisses weren't enough to base a long-term love affair on. It should be easy to end it now rather than drag it out and make them both miserable.

THE NEXT DAY, he was running late and purposely ignored the home next door. He drove right by without slowing or checking to see if Collette's car had made it out of the driveway.

Granted, he could see in his peripheral vision that it had. Truth was, if her car had still been there, he'd have stopped to help.

His assistance hadn't been needed.

Hope hadn't texted him, asking him to let her know when he'd be home, making it easier for him to ignore the daughter as well as the mother.

The day went by without a hint of either of the McCallick women interrupting his thoughts.

Much.

It helped to stay busy working out, testing communications equipment and reviewing current events in foreign nations. If he were lucky, they'd get the word before the weekend that they were needed to extract a political figure or blow up a bridge somewhere far away from Killeen, Texas, and the one redhead who had captured his thoughts. Only his thoughts. It was too soon for her to own his heart.

Wasn't it?

The day ended without a call to rescue anyone. No spewing faucets, druggies demanding their stuff back or drunks making moves on a woman who didn't appreciate his attentions. Obviously, Collette had no interest in him other than as a plumber, mechanic and bodyguard.

He checked his cellphone the next day and then the next one after that. No calls from his neighbor or her daughter. Was she on the same mission as he was...to eradicate any feelings for the person living next door?

Good. That would make it even easier to forget her. Without the constant reminder, he'd be able to get on with his life.

That was if he actually had a life.

Friday came and went. He avoided going to the Salty Dog Saloon, knowing she would be there. He'd driven by it that night and had nearly succumbed to temptation. When he'd slowed to turn into the parking lot, a kid in a BMW had honked at him to hurry up.

The sound had brought him back to reality. Instead of turning into the parking lot, he'd continued driving straight, irritating the crap out of the BMW crawling up his tailpipe.

On Saturday, he accepted an invitation to Rucker and Nora's place for a barbeque.

"You can bring your plus one," Rucker had said.

"What plus one?" John had asked.

"That waitress at the Salty Dog. You seemed pretty interested in her. Was her name Colleen?"

"Collette," John corrected.

"That's the one." Rucker grinned. "Why don't you ask her out?"

John shook his head. "Not interested."

"You or her?" Rucker asked.

"Both."

"Then come by yourself." Rucker's grin broadened. "Or, I can see if Nora has a nurse friend she can fix you up with."

John glared at his team lead. "Don't do me any favors. I'm happiest alone."

"That's what you say when you don't want to make the effort anymore," Rucker laughed. "Okay, I'll tell Nora to hold off on finding you a date. But say the word, and she'll do her best."

He'd gone to Rucker and Nora's place, stayed long enough to realize he was miserable and left after dark had settled over Texas.

Back at his camper, he had no desire to sit in the fake leather lounger and put his feet up like some old man out to pasture for the rest of his life.

Instead of relaxing, John put on his shorts, running shoes and tank top and went for a two-mile run, which stretched into four, then six and then eight. By the time he finally made it back to his camper, another vehicle was parked in Collette's driveway.

Collette would be working that night at the Salty Dog Saloon.

John worried that Hope was home alone with whomever owned the white sedan parked next to their home. He considered knocking on their door and demanding to know who had invaded their space.

Halfway around the end of the trailer, he heard voices coming from inside.

When he rounded the corner, he froze, and then stepped out of sight.

Hope and her boyfriend Ryan were coming out of the trailer and heading for the sedan. Ryan held the door for Hope as she slipped into the passenger seat.

Once she was settled, the young man rounded the front of the car and climbed into the driver's seat. Ryan drove away with Hope. Probably on a date. Hopefully, Sly wouldn't recognize them in this different vehicle and try to destroy it like he'd done Ryan's truck.

John sat outside in his folding chair with his head tipped back, staring up at the stars.

He must have fallen to sleep, because he woke with a start when a bug landed on his forehead.

When he pushed to his feet, he glanced down at his watch. Hell, he'd been sitting in that chair for a few hours. He rolled his head around, popping the kinks out of his neck.

Collette would be home soon. Ryan's car wasn't in the drive, and no lights were lit inside the trailer. Wasn't it a little late for Hope to be out? For several minutes, he debated calling Collette. After another minute and a half, he called the number he'd saved to his cellphone.

"John, are you all right?" Collette's voice came across with loud music in the background.

"I am, but I don't think Hope's home. Isn't it late for her to be out?"

"She shouldn't be home. She went with the church youth club to a waterpark today. They're staying the night at a hotel with loads of chaperones, and then visiting the Alamo tomorrow. She won't be back until tomorrow evening."

"Okay," John said, feeling foolish. "Glad to hear she's having fun. Sorry to bother you."

"You're not bothering me. I should be heading home soon. Thank you for caring enough about Hope to call me."

"You're welcome. Have a great day."

"John?" Collette's voice stilled his hand. "Did I say something to make you mad?"

"I don't know what you're talking about," he stalled. He had no excuse for his behavior. He'd really tried hard to ignore her and had thought he was managing quite well. When he heard her voice, all his willpower flew out the window.

"What are you doing after work?" he asked.

"Putting my feet up," she said and moaned. "What I'd really like is a glass of wine and a view of the stars."

"I think I can arrange that," John said. "I have the chairs, and I can pick up some wine. Anything in particular?"

"Go cheap. I'm used to it. I'll pay you back. I should be there in thirty minutes." She ended the call.

John jumped into his truck and raced to the nearest liquor store that was still open and bought a bottle of Collette's favorite wine and a six-pack of his beer. He was back at the camper in less than fifteen minutes.

For the next twenty minutes, he cleaned he camper, putting away as much of his junk as he could. He made the bed and stood back admiring his attempt to make his temporary home more cheerful and less cluttered.

Moments later, Collette pulled into the trailer park and parked beside her trailer. She climbed out of her car and stretched.

John joined her beside her vehicle. "Hey."

She stared up at him with a soft smile. "Hey, yourself."

"What can I do to help out?"

"I want to get a quick shower. Then I'll join you out here."

He stepped back, allowing her to pass him and enter her home. She walked through the door and closed it behind her.

Less than a second later, she reopened the door and stared out at him. "There is something you can do for me."

"What's that?" he asked.

"Soap my back."

John blinked. "What?"

"You heard me. I want you to help me by soaping my back." She lifted her chin. "Unless I read you wrong, and you're really not interested."

"As in rub soap over your body?" he asked.

She smiled. "Yes. In the shower, getting wet and... naked."

His brow dipped. "Are you sure?"

Collette nodded. "I've been dreaming about it."

"So have I," he admitted, taking a tentative step toward her. "What about your stance on relationships?"

Her smile slipped, and her expression turned serious. "I'm not asking for forever."

John took another step forward. "We live next to each other. Will this make it awkward?"

Collette shrugged. "Any more awkward than we are now, standing on the porch, talking about *it* and not actually doing *it*?"

John climbed the porch steps and stood in front of her, wanting her more than he'd ever imagined wanting a woman, but afraid that if they took the next step...

What? They might enjoy making love? They might want to do it again?

Collette touched a hand to his chest. "We both have our reasons for keeping things commitment-free. Yet, there's an undeniable attraction brewing." She looked up into his eyes. "At least on my side."

"And mine." He raised a hand to cup her cheek. "You're beautiful. I find my control slipping every time I'm near you."

She laid her hand over his and turned her face into his palm. "Then let it go." Her lips pressed against his skin, sending a powerful wave of desire raging throughout his body.

"If I step through that door, there's no going back," he warned.

"Good. I wouldn't have invited you in if I wasn't sure." She took his hand in hers and pulled him through the door into the trailer.

While he closed the door behind them and twisted the lock, she pulled her blouse over her head and let it fall to the floor.

Collette stood in a pair of short denim shorts

frayed around her thighs and a lacy black bra. She backed toward the hallway leading to her bathroom, crooking her finger as she went, a sexy smile curling her lips.

John ripped his T-shirt over his head, flung it against the wall and stalked her like a cat on the prowl.

She paused long enough to shimmy out of her shorts, kicking them to the side. Then she turned, displaying the rounded curves of her butt cheeks.

The woman wore thong panties.

John groaned, his cock hardening to concrete, pushing against the thick denim of his jeans. He ripped open the button, yanked down his zipper and let his aching shaft free.

Collette stopped at the doorway to the bathroom and cast a glance over her shoulder, a smile spreading across her face. "Commando?"

"Damn right," he growled. He toed off his boots and kicked free of them, one at a time. He plucked his wallet out of his back pocket, found a condom within and tossed the wallet on an end table. Then his jeans were off, and he stood completely naked.

He closed the distance between them, taking her into his arms. "Sweet Jesus, you're gorgeous." He bent to nibble the sensitive skin along the side of her neck and inhaled the scent of her shampoo. Honeysuckle. It brought images to mind of her lying amongst honeysuckle vines, the flowers and greenery an apt contrast to her pale skin and fiery red hair.

Her leg slipped around the back of his calf and slid upward until her sex rubbed the top of his thigh.

John's breath lodged in his throat; his pulse hammered through his veins. If he didn't make love to her soon, he'd break apart into a million pieces.

Collette reached up behind her and unclasped her bra.

John eased the straps down her shoulders and let the garment fall to the floor.

Then he hooked his thumbs into the waistband of her panties and dragged them over her thighs and downward, running his hands over the silky skin of her inner thighs. He lowered his tall frame to follow the path of her panties.

She shifted, widening her stance, her hands weaving into his short-cropped hair.

John paused to press his lips to her belly, and then to the tuft of hair over her sex. He flicked his tongue against her inner thigh as his fingers pulled the panties free of her ankles.

As he rose, he cupped her sex and pressed gently with one hand while the other found her breast.

She leaned into him, her chest rising on a deeply indrawn breath. Collette circled her hands around the back of his neck and brought his lips down to hers. She initiated the kiss, gnawed on his lips and thrust her tongue past his teeth to slide the length of his.

John liked that she took charge and showed him what she liked in a kiss. He hoped she'd take it further and show him what she liked when making love.

Collette took his hand and led him to the shower, turned on the water and kissed him again while she waited for the water to warm. Then she stepped beneath the spray.

He followed, depositing the condom on the counter, within reach of the shower. Reaching for the bar of soap on the edge of the tub, he held it beneath the spray and worked up a bubbly lather.

Then Collette took the bar from him and lathered her hands as well.

They came together, touching each other, running their hands over every inch of skin.

John liked her soft, yet firm, fingers on his arms, shoulders and torso. His breath caught and held as she worked her way downward to where his cock stood at attention, hot, thick and hard as stone.

Her hands circled him there, warm and strong.

John gripped her shoulders, his body already halfway there. He had to control his reaction to her attentions, or it would all be over too soon.

Collette slid her hands up and down his shaft, slowly at first. With each pass, her speed increased.

John matched her rhythm, thrusting into her grip. As the tension increased, so too did his need to hold back. He wanted her to feel every bit as amazing as she was making him feel before they took it all the way.

As he neared the edge, he pulled free of her hands and stepped back.

When she looked at him, he shook his head. "Not yet."

He turned her into the spray, quickly rinsing the soap from her body, then slipped beneath the showerhead, washed away the bubbles from his skin and turned off the water.

"Done already?" she asked, reaching for a towel.

"Not even close." He moved her wet hair to one side and nuzzled her neck. "We've only just begun."

Collette leaned her head to one side and moaned. "Mmm. I'm glad."

Taking his time, he dried her from head to toe, stopping to taste her along the way and lingering on her breasts.

Collette did the same, pressing kisses to his chest, his abdomen, and she would have gone lower, but he couldn't risk it. Not yet. He had work to do to make her as hot as he was.

When they were both dry, he scooped her up in his arms, snagged the condom from where he'd left it on the counter and edged through the doorway into her bedroom. With little room to maneuver, he laid her on the full-sized bed and dropped down beside her.

"I need a bigger bed," she said, running her fingers along the side of his cheek and down the length of his neck.

"You need a bigger house." He kissed her, thinking of the master bedroom he'd designed in his house. Within the next two months, he'd be in it. He couldn't wait to take her there.

Inch by inch, he trailed his lips across her skin, starting with her mouth then working his way downward to the pulse beating at the base of her throat. Moving still lower, he skimmed across her collar bone and downward to take one of her breasts into his hand. With careful attention to her reactions, he flicked the nipple with the tip of his tongue.

Her back arched off the mattress and fell back.

He flicked it again, and she arched again.

When he took the nipple between his teeth and rolled it gently, she writhed beneath him and moaned.

He grinned and worked the other breast, giving it equal time and care, before he moved lower, skimming his lips across her ribs, dipping into her belly button and pausing at her mound.

She parted her legs, allowing him to position himself between them. John draped her knees over his shoulders, parted her folds and lowered his mouth to within an inch of his goal.

Collette pulled her knees up, and her hands bunched in the fabric of the comforter, her body tensing.

John started by blowing a warm stream of air over her clit.

Her chest rose with a quickly indrawn breath.

He flicked the nubbin of flesh with the tip of his tongue.

Her head came up off the pillow. "There," she breathed.

With a grin, he flicked her again.

She threw back her head and moaned. "Again."

John complied. Flicking once, and then sucking her clit between his teeth and nibbling gently.

Collette gasped. "Sweet heaven."

Now that he had her attention, he flicked, licked and stroked her again and again, until her hips rose off the mattress, and her body stiffened. Her release came fast. She rocked with the waves, her fingers twisting into his hair, holding him close until he'd milked her for everything.

When she fell back onto the mattress, she breathed several ragged breaths then gripped his shoulders and dragged him up her body. "I want you. Inside. Now."

He grabbed for the packet he'd tossed onto the comforter and ripped it open.

Collette took the condom from him and rolled it over his engorged shaft, all the way down to the base.

She paused to fondle his balls, squeezing them gently between her fingers. Then she wrapped her hands around his hips and guided him to her entrance.

With his cock nudging her, he could feel the warmth of her juices. With extreme care, he pressed into her. If he was right, she hadn't had sex with a man in some time. Based on how tightly she fit around him...a long time. He'd only just entered, when her fingers dug into his ass, and she pulled hard, shooting him all the way home.

For a long moment, he remained buried inside her without moving, allowing her to adjust to his girth.

When he felt she was ready, he pulled almost all the way out.

Again, her fingers dug into his ass and she slammed him back home.

"Faster," she urged.

He chuckled. "Impatient?"

She inhaled and released the air. "On fire."

Complying with her demands, he moved in and out, increasing his speed with each thrust until he was pounding like the piston in a car's engine.

His body tensed, the sensations building, until he shot over the edge, his release coming fast and hard, shaking him to the very core. One last thrust sent him deep inside where he remained, his cock pulsing to an internal rhythm, leaving him feeling so primal he wanted to beat his chest and shout in the wind.

He rode the wave all the way to the end, collapsing on top of her when his arms would hold him no longer. Gathering her in his embrace, he rolled to the side and held her. Still connected. Still wrapped in the aftermath of the most earthshattering experience he'd encountered.

Collette touched her lips to his chest and sighed. "Wow. If sex is like that every time, I've been missing out all these years. My vibrator doesn't begin to hold a candle to that."

His cock twitched inside her. "You own a vibrator?" The thought of all he could do with her and a vibrator…

She twirled a finger around one of his hard brown nipples. "A girl has needs."

He captured her finger in his hand and brought it to his lips. "Save that thought and your vibrator for when I have the energy for an encore."

"Mmm. I like the way you think." She pressed her cheek to his chest and relaxed against him. "Hope was right."

He laughed. "About what?"

"A lot of things. But about just getting on with what was right there in front of us."

"Our mutual attraction?"

Collette nodded. "If it was obvious to a sixteen-year-old, why wasn't it obvious to us?"

"We were too busy fighting the attraction." He smoothed her damp hair back behind her ear.

She closed her eyes on a sigh. "I'm glad we surrendered."

With her body pressed to his, and his cock still thick and encased in her warmth, John couldn't agree more.

He just worried what the next day might bring.

Would she regret their decision to succumb to their attraction?

John had no regrets.

CHAPTER 9

COLLETTE LOVED HAVING John in her bed that night and halfway through the next day. Hunger drove them out of bed and the trailer in search of sustenance.

They sat outside on his camp chairs for lunch, enjoying the shade on a hot Texas day, sipping iced tea and eating sandwiches of deli meat, lettuce and tomatoes.

"I don't get outside enough," Collette commented.

"I get out all the time. You'd think I would spend all my off time indoors."

"That might be too confining for a man who's larger than life." Collette polished off the last bite of her sandwich and leaned back in her chair, letting the warm arm air lull her into such a relaxed state she felt like her bones had melted.

John chuckled. "Larger than life?" He grinned. "I like the sound of that."

"Well, larger than me and much too big to live in a camp trailer for very long."

"Hopefully, they'll finish my house before too long," he said, staring out over the farmland beyond the trailer park. "I look forward to living there, raising cattle and horses. I might even get a dog and a barn cat. Guess I'll have to look into building a barn next."

"You need a barn if you're planning on having a barn cat." Her heart was heavy at the thought of John leaving within the next two months. "You'll be happy with more room to move around inside." And she'd be sad that she wouldn't see him coming out of his camper in the morning carrying a cup of coffee, looking all buff and manly in his uniform. Collette sighed. "Hope will miss you."

"Hope?" He turned toward her, and eyebrow cocked. "What about you?"

She forced a casual shrug. "Maybe a little."

He pushed to his feet, took her hand and dragged her out of her chair.

"Hey, I was almost asleep."

"You'll miss me a little?" He crushed her body against his and lowered his head until his lips hovered over hers. "I'll miss holding you like this." John claimed her lips in a sensuous kiss that took her breath away. "I'll miss kissing you like that," he said when his mouth finally left hers. He brushed the hair back from her forehead and lowered his voice to a whisper. "And I'll miss the way your eyes sparkle and your cheeks flush when we're making love."

Her pulse kicked into highspeed. "Let me show you some sparkle and flush." She took his hand and started for her trailer.

As she rounded the corner to the front, a white sedan pulled into the park and came to a stop behind her car.

Hope and Ryan leaped out. "Holy smokes, Mom. We were only gone overnight, and Sly's been at it again."

Collette reluctantly released John's hand and pulled her daughter into her arms. "Are you two okay?"

"We're fine, but Sly and his bunch trashed Ryan's house. His parents are sick about it. You should see it. They'll have to hire someone to power wash the brick and clean paint off the windows. There's no way they'll get it off themselves."

"Whoa, slow down." Collette stepped back and turned to Ryan. "Sly and his gang got paint on your folks' place?"

"Yes, ma'am," Ryan said in his quiet tone, the flare of his pupils the only indication he was angry. "They spray-painted graffiti all over the house."

"Bastards," John muttered.

"They did it in the early hours of the morning,"

Hope said. "Ryan's folks were in Dallas for the weekend. They came home this morning to find the mess. We stopped by to see the damage after we left the church. I can't believe that asshole is getting away with everything he's done."

"You have to catch him in the act," John said. "Did your folks have a security system that might've caught a face on camera?"

Ryan shook his head. "They've never needed one. It's only been since Mark disappeared that they started locking their doors at night."

"Did they report it to the police?" Collette asked, her arm still around her daughter.

"Yes, ma'am," Ryan responded. "They came, took pictures and wrote a report."

"But without eyewitnesses, or fingerprints on spray cans, the police don't have much to go on," John concluded.

The teen nodded his head. "Exactly. My folks are tired of the threats and living in fear. My brother doesn't realize how his actions are affecting the rest of us. I'm sure that if he knew, he'd find a way to stop Sly."

"And you have no idea where Mark is?" John asked.

Ryan sighed. "No, sir."

"At least you weren't run off the road again." Collette hugged Hope, anger burning inside. She felt helpless. What could she do to make Sly stop terrorizing good people?

"I thought they'd given up on bothering Ryan and his family," Hope said. "I guess I was wrong."

"Which makes me afraid for you and Ryan," Collette said. "I don't like the idea of you riding your bike to school until Sly is brought to justice. I'll drop you off on my way to class."

"What about after school? I ride my bike to the library or the church."

"I can get you there on my way to work," Ryan said. "It's on my way."

"And I can pick you up on my way home," Collette said. "I don't want you walking or riding your bike alone until Sly's dealt with."

"Mom, I can take care of myself," Hope protested.

"Humor me." Collette pulled her into another hug. "You're all I've got."

"I'm not going anywhere," Hope said. "At least until I go to college."

"And I want to make sure you live long enough to get your degree and a job. Someone has to take care of me in my old age."

"Mom." Hope rolled her eyes. "You're not getting old."

"I will someday. You're my long-term care plan." She winked. "We'll muddle through this situation the best we can."

"What about when you have to work on a weeknight?"

John held up a hand. "I can pick her up from the church or library on those nights, as long as I'm not deployed anytime soon."

Collette smiled. "Thank you, John." She turned to Hope. "Is that okay with you?"

"Anytime I get to ride shotgun in Mr. Sanders's badass truck is fine with me." She grinned at John, her gaze going from him back to her mother, her eyes narrowing. "Something's different."

Collette's cheeks heated. "I don't know what you're talking about. Are you hungry?"

"Always," Hope said.

"I've got sandwich meat in my camper," John offered. "We just finished eating lunch."

"I'll make the sandwiches." Collette headed for John's camper. They'd been in and out of her trailer and his camper enough she felt comfortable making herself at home in either.

"I'll help," Hope said, following her.

Once inside the tiny kitchen, Hope pinned her mother with her piercing gaze. "What's up with you and Mr. Sanders?"

"Nothing," Collette focused her attention on the refrigerator as she pulled out deli meat and condiments.

"Liar." Hope crossed her arms over her chest.

"Something's changed. *You're* different." Her eyes narrowed as she studied Collette.

"I'm your mother. Always have been. Always will be. Now, what do you want on your sandwich?"

Her daughter continued to stare at her, making her squirm in her own skin. Then her frown disappeared, and her eyes widened. "Holy smokes, Mom, you did it, didn't you? You and Mr. Sanders did it." She clapped her hands. "I knew it. You two had googly eyes for each other ever since you met." She hugged her mother. "I'm happy for you. You needed it."

Collette laughed, her cheeks hot, her blood on fire. John had a way of doing that to her. She raised a finger to her lips. "Shh. What us adults do is none of your business."

"Come on, Mom. I'm not a small child. I've known about the birds and the bees since I was eleven."

Collette gasped. "What? I'm almost certain I didn't tell you any such thing. Not at that age."

Hope shook her head. "You didn't have to. My friends were happy to educate me with the pamphlets their parents were handing them. We would crowd under our sheet tents in our bedrooms and go over everything, giggling at the pictures and imagining our male classmates' anatomies. Those pamphlets were very informative and made their rounds at school several times."

Collette shook her head. "And here I thought you were an innocent little girl." She layered thin slices of turkey and roast beef on bread, added lettuce and tomatoes, a squirt of mayo and mustard and closed with another slice of bread. While she worked, she began to realize just how grown up her little girl was. She had to remind herself that she'd been sixteen when she'd gotten pregnant. Seventeen by the time she'd had her baby and had become a mother.

She turned to Hope and gripped her shoulders. "Please, if you have learned anything from me, I hope you've learned from my mistakes. I know you'll experiment with sex, just be careful."

Hope smiled gently. "I wouldn't be here but for your *mistake.* So, I can't call it a mistake. Don't worry, Mom. Ryan and I haven't gone past necking in the front seat of his truck. Which is in the shop. It feels weird going on dates in his parent's car. I just can't do anything in it." She shuddered. "I'll be glad when his truck is fixed, and we can go out in it."

"Do I need to set up an appointment with our doctor to get you on birth control pills?" Collette asked.

This time, Hope blushed. "No, Mom. I did that myself. I have a prescription I've been using now for the past six months."

"Since you turned sixteen?" Collette shook her head. "Where was I? Have I been burying my head in the sand while my little girl has been growing up and taking charge of her own health and wellbeing?" Tears welled in her eyes. "I'm a terrible mother."

Hope frowned. "No, you're not. You're the best. And you're working hard to make your life and mine better. You're setting the best example for me to follow."

"Except for the part about getting pregnant at sixteen." Collette gave her daughter a hug. "I love you and don't regret a single thing about keeping you. My parents wanted me to give you up for adoption. I couldn't. I'm glad I didn't."

"So am I." Hope hugged her back, and then stepped away. "Now, let's get these sandwiches outside before I start crying. I like Mr. Sanders. If you two fall in love, you have my blessing."

Collette brushed a tear from her cheek as she watched her grown daughter carry sandwiches out to her boyfriend. She didn't regret a day of Hope's life.

As she descended the narrow steps of the camper, her gaze went to John Sanders and a smile curled the corners of her lips. She didn't regret making love with the man. If they only had a day, a week, two months or a year together, it was better than nothing.

Hope liked him. Her approval meant the world to Collette. Her daughter had good taste.

What wasn't to like? The man was strong, handy with tools and sexy as hell.

If she wasn't careful, she would fall in love with him. If she'd learned one thing by having a baby before finishing high school, happily-ever-after was stuff fairytales were made of. She should be satisfied with happy-for-now.

John's brow creased. "Everything all right?"

"Yes," she said. *For now.*

OVER THE FOLLOWING WEEK, John spent his days at Fort Hood training with his team and his evenings watching the sunsets with Collette and, sometimes, Hope.

Without her bicycle, Hope depended on Collette to collect her from the library or the church every afternoon after her mother got out of nursing school.

On Thursday, John got a text from Collette.

Collette: Sarge needs me to work tonight after I get out of school. Are you available to pick up Hope at the church?

John: No problem. I'll be there around four-forty-five

Collette: Thank you. I owe you.

He wanted to tell her she didn't owe him anything, but she'd argue the point. Her independence was important to her. He'd miss their evening watching the sunset after doing so every night of the week so far. They could start a tradition of watching the sunrises on Saturday and Sunday. Otherwise, it might be Sunday before they could spend time together again, unless he just happened to hang out at the Salty Dog Thursday and Friday night. He'd promised to watch football with the team at Bull's place on Saturday and he could go to the Salty Dog that night as well.

With Hope home every night, he and Collette kept their conversations and actions nonsexual. Apparently, Collette's daughter had figured out they'd made love while she'd been away. Collette didn't want to embarrass Hope with overt displays of affection. That didn't stop John from sneaking a kiss in the dark when Hope had gone to bed. He didn't want to push the issue, knowing Collette needed to focus on her work and Hope's safety.

He was glad to help by getting Hope home from the church. He'd even make sure she ate dinner by cooking a pot of chili. That way she wouldn't have to be alone in the trailer all evening, and he could sit outside and enjoy the night air with good company.

Hope was a lot like her mother. At the same time, she was her own individual. He liked her. Even more, he liked her mother.

A lot.

So much so, he could see them sitting on the swing on the porch of his house in the country, watching the sun set on the horizon every night for the rest of their lives.

He'd be damned if he wasn't falling in love with Collette McCallick.

Rucker crossed to where he sat in the armory

after getting the text from Collette. "What's got my buddy Tank frowning like someone just kicked your dog?"

"I don't have a dog," Tank grumbled. Love? Was he really falling in love with Collette? He wished Rucker would go away and let him chew on this new feeling.

"Seriously, man. You can talk to me. Someone piss you off?"

"You love Nora, right?" Tank burst out before he could form a reasonable thought.

Rucker leaned back, his eyebrows forming a V. "Yes. I do. Why do you ask?"

"When did you fall in love with her?"

Rucker's lips spread across his face in a wide smile. "Not long after we met. I just didn't realize it at the time because I was so convinced love and marriage wasn't for me. Why do you ask?" His eyes widened. "You've got a woman."

"No, I don't," John disagreed vehemently. Then he thought of the night they'd spent together making love and the ones they'd held hands watching the sunset. He'd been just as happy holding her hand in silence, drinking in the beauty of nature and the feel of her hand in his. He sighed. "I guess I do. Sort of."

Rucker's face broke out in a grin, and he shouted, "Hey, guys! Tank's got a woman!"

Dash was the first to reach him and pound him on the back. "Son of a bitch, what poor woman was dumb enough to fall for you?"

Bull was next. His slaps on the back sent Tank staggering forward. "Didn't see that coming. Who is she?"

"I bet it's the redheaded waitress from the Salty Dog," Mac said. "He was eyeing her like a side of beef at Dawg and Beth's engagement party."

"Redhead?" Blade glared at Tank. "Don't go poaching on my redhead. Sophia's my woman."

Mac backhanded Blade in the belly. "Not that redhead. The waitress who kicked Joe's ass."

"If she can put that asshole Joe in his place, she can put up with Tank." Dawg clapped a hand on Tank's back. "Congratulations, dude. I thought you were waiting until you retired to find someone."

"When you find the right one, you can't let her get away." Lance shook Tank's hand instead of pounding on his back, for which Tank was grateful.

Mac snorted. "Lance, what do you know about women? You're the last man standing without one."

"I just know," Lance grumbled. "Anyway, you're missing the point. Tank's got someone."

"Thanks," John said. "But I'm not sure I have her."

"What do you mean?" Rucker asked.

"I mean, I like her and all, but I'm not sure she wants anything permanent." He shoved a hand through his hair, hating that the guys now knew he was interested in Collette. They'd tease him relentlessly. "And I told her that I wasn't in the market for a relationship until I retire from the Army."

"That's what you always told us," Mac said. "But how many of us said the same thing? Delta's have a high divorce rate. Women want a man at home, not gone 365 days a year."

"So, how is it Kylie Adams fell for your ugly mug?" Bull asked. "Or Nora for Rucker?"

"They understand deployment," Rucker said. "Then there's Layla."

Bull frowned. "What about her?"

"She knows what she's getting into with you, and yet she chooses to be part of your life," Rucker said.

"She grew up in the State Department with her father being an ambassador and all. She knows the sacrifices our military men make," Bull said.

"Sophia didn't grow up in the military, nor is she serving," Blade said.

Rucker nodded. "What all our women have in common is that they're strong, independent and kickass. They don't need us." He paused. "They choose to be with us and can function on their own without us around."

Bull nodded. "We're damned lucky."

John thought about the women his teammates had in their lives. Each one of the men had been against long-term relationships, either because they'd been burned before or had watched other Deltas suffer when their wives left them. John was no different. He hadn't wanted to get involved. Once burned, and all.

"Your woman is like ours in that respect," Rucker said. "We heard what she did to subdue Joe. I wish we'd been there to see that."

"If you're serious about her, you need to tell her," Mac said. "Don't let her get away without telling her how you feel. She might think she doesn't want to live with the complications of being with a Delta, but if she loves you, she won't want to live without you."

"That's right. You have to give her the choice," Blade said.

John grimaced. "We just started seeing each other."

"At the Salty Dog?" Bull asked.

John shook his head. "No. She's actually my neighbor at the trailer park."

Blade gave John a crooked grin. "You know Sophia and I started out that way. Friends and neighbors. It took a trip to Cancun and an altercation with a drug cartel for me to realize I loved her."

"So, what are you waiting for?" Dawg asked.

"Time for us to get to know each other," John said. "I've only known her two weeks tops."

"When you know…" Mac started.

"You know," Bull finished.

"Yeah, but I don't want to scare her away." John paced away from his teammates, turned and came back. "Look, don't say anything to her at the Salty Dog. I need to take this at my own pace."

Lance snorted. "Glacial, I'd bet."

"She has a daughter to think about."

"A little girl?" Rucker grinned. "A ready-made family. That's awesome."

John shook his head. "Not a little girl. She's sixteen and, strangely, an old soul." He looked up at Rucker. "You'd like her. And you'd all like Collette."

"The redhead has a name." Mac raised an imaginary beer. "To Collette!"

Dash shook his head. "Let's celebrate at the Salty Dog tonight with a real beer and maybe the woman of the hour...?"

"No can do," John glanced at his watch. "I need to go. I have to pick up her daughter and get her home. Collette is working tonight."

Dawg gave him a sly grin. "At the Salty Dog?"

"Yes." John's eyes narrowed. "I'm serious. I don't know where we're going or if she's even that into me."

Rucker stepped forward. "In other words, be cool. Don't screw it up for him." He shot a stern look at Dawg and every other man on the team. "We're a team. We look out for each other. If Tank wants this to work, we have to help."

"By not helping," Tank added.

"Okay," Dawg said. "But we can still hang out at the saloon. I could use a beer."

"As long as you don't do or say anything to Collette," Tank warned.

"Can I order a beer?" Dawg asked.

Bull threw a cleaning rag at Dawg. "Don't be an ass."

"What?" Dawg said. "She might be our waitress."

"Be cool." Rucker turned to Tank. "I'll go with him and stuff my fist in his mouth if he does something stupid."

"And I'll go to check out this redhead," Lance said.

"Hey," Tank said. "No poaching."

Lance grinned. "You aren't married yet. She's fair game."

Rucker sighed. "I'll put a leash on Lance." He waved at Tank. "Go. I've got your back."

"We all do," Dawg said. "We just have to poke the bear for fun."

Tank shook his head. "With friends like you, I don't need enemies. I'll see you all in the morning." He left, regretting saying anything to his team. He'd be sweating bullets all evening, worrying about what the guys might be doing or saying to Collette at the Salty Dog. He wished he could be there to make sure they didn't say anything about his confession.

First things first, though.

Hope.

She needed someone to pick her up before they locked the doors at the church.

He hurried out to his truck, drove off post and sped through Killeen, cursing at the red lights and speeding to the next intersection, only to be stopped again. It was a minute after five o'clock when he pulled into the parking lot of the church. The lot was empty but for one dirty white van.

John kicked himself for being a minute late. He hadn't wanted Collette's daughter to worry that he'd forgotten.

Hope leaned against the wide front doors that led into the chapel, her backpack slung over one shoulder.

John parked and dropped down from the driver's seat. "Hey," he said with a smile. "Sorry I'm late."

"You're fine." Hope pushed away from the door and walked toward him. "The secretaries just left. I told them they didn't have to wait for my ride to come. I knew you'd be here. They had to get home to feed their families."

A movement at the far corner of the church complex caught John's attention. He glanced toward a big man exiting a smaller door. He wore a gray coverall and carried what appeared to be a toolbox. He glanced their way, his gaze going to Hope first, and then John. Then he hurried toward the white van without making further eye contact. The guy was strange.

"Who's that?" John asked as the van drove past his truck and turned out onto street.

"That's the janitor, Mr. Earles." Hope shivered. "He gives me the creeps. I swear he's always looking at me. I'll be studying in one of the Sunday school rooms, and I'll look up and he's standing in the doorway. When I see him, he shuffles off without saying a word to me. I think he might be mental or something. They must have felt sorry for him when they hired him to clean the church. He's always here. I see his van parked outside even when no one else is here."

John opened the passenger door for her.

Hope climbed in and turned to John with a frown. "Do you think he lives here? I mean, maybe he can't afford a place of his own on what they pay him."

John shrugged. "I don't know. It does seem strange. You might consider hanging out at the library if he makes you feel uncomfortable. There are probably more people there."

She nodded.

John closed the door, rounded the front of the truck and slid behind the steering wheel. "Feel like getting a burger?"

She shook her head. "Not really. I'm saving my allowance for Saturday night. The youth group is having a marathon movie night. We're staying out until midnight."

"Is your mother on board with that?" John asked as he pulled out of the parking lot onto the street leading to the main drag through Killeen.

"Sure. She's all for participation with the youth group. They're well-chaperoned and clean fun. It's better than hanging out at the lake, getting drunk, which is what most of the kids my age do."

"Good point." He'd been one of those kids out drinking with his friends, underage and stupid. They'd been lucky to live through that phase. A few kids in his high school hadn't been as fortunate.

He turned into the mobile home park, coming to a stop beside his camper.

Hope was out of the truck before he could open the door for her.

"Thanks for giving me a ride home," she said and headed for her trailer.

"I'm making chili tonight if you care to join me," he called out.

"I have homework."

"You can bring it. I won't talk. I prefer not to eat alone."

She paused, her brow furrowing when she turned to look back at him. "Did my mother put you up to feeding me?"

He grinned. "No. I really like having someone share a meal with me."

"You could ask old man Randolph. Chili might work for him. He doesn't have any teeth."

John tried again. "I don't know him. And I like your company."

She tilted her head. "Why?"

He laughed. "You challenge me. I have to be on my toes in a conversation with you."

Her eyes narrowed. "Some people find that irritating."

"I'm not some people." He turned away. "The offer stands. Dinner should be ready in an hour. We can eat in silence if you like. I only know how to make enough for ten people. You'd be doing me a favor by eating a healthy portion. My refrigerator isn't big enough for a lot of leftovers."

Her mouth twisted into a skeptical smile. "You really like my mother, don't you?"

He didn't deny her statement, choosing to counter with a question of his own. "What does that have to do with chili?"

"You're trying too hard to ingratiate yourself with me." She sighed. "You don't have to work so hard. You already have my approval." She left him standing there.

A moment later, he heard the door to her trailer open and close. Through the window into the kitchen, he could see her moving around.

Hope was an old soul. She needed to learn how to be young and carefree. Then again, that was how he'd been. She might not be wired the same.

All he knew was that he liked her and really hoped she'd join him for chili.

However, he'd better get cooking or there wouldn't be any chili.

An hour later, he sat at the outdoor camp table with two bowls of chili.

Alone.

He was on his second spoonful when the

redhaired teen appeared in T-shirts and shorts and took the chair opposite him.

He didn't say a word, just ate in silence with the daughter of the woman he found himself loving more and more each day.

Her mother had raised an intelligent, independent young woman with enough grit to make it in life.

When she'd finished her chili, she helped him clean the dishes.

As she turned to leave, she asked, "Would you mind picking me up from the library tomorrow afternoon?"

"No problem," he said.

"Thanks for dinner." Hope hurried back to the trailer.

When John was sure she was inside and safe, he moved his camp chair to a position where he could watch the sunset. It wasn't the same as when he sat with Collette, holding her hand, but it was peaceful and gave him time to reflect on his interactions with Hope and Collette and the reaction he'd gotten from his team upon learning he had a thing for a woman. They were happy for him, despite the teasing.

As for Hope, it might be too late for him to be a father figure to her, but he could learn to be her friend.

He'd like that and hoped his relationship with Collette gave him that chance.

Collette.

Strong, loyal, caring and sexy as hell. She had goals and ambition. She also wasn't the type who'd ditch him while he was deployed. He could see himself growing old with her.

Yeah, he was thinking of a future with a woman, who came as a package deal, while he was still a member of Delta Force. The beauty of it was that the thought no longer scared the shit out of him.

CHAPTER 10

WHEN COLLETTE RETURNED HOME after ten o'clock Thursday night, she went straight to Hope's room to kiss her goodnight.

"How was your evening?" she asked, bending over her daughter's bed to press her lips to her forehead.

"Good."

Collette sat on the edge of the bed. "Did you find something for dinner?"

Hope yawned and stretched. "Chili."

"Chili?" Collette tipped her head. "Where did you get chili?"

"Your boyfriend." Hope rolled onto her side and tucked her hand beneath her cheek. "He's a good guy. You could do worse." She closed her eyes. "Night, Mom. Love you."

"Night, sweetie." Collette turned off the light on

her daughter's nightstand, left her room and closed the door behind her.

Boyfriend? Since when was John her boyfriend? She hadn't corrected Hope since she'd been half-asleep when she'd called John her boyfriend. Who else would have fed her chili on a hot Texas day?

Boyfriends were what you had in high school. John wasn't her boyfriend. He was her friend.

In the back of her mind, a little voice interjected. *He's more than that, and you know it.*

Yeah, he was. Collette just wasn't ready to put a name to what they were to each other. She'd only survived in her life by remaining focused on what was important.

Her daughter.

Everything she'd done for the past sixteen years had been geared toward making sure Hope had food, clothes and a roof over her head. Now that she was becoming more self-sufficient, Collette had a little more time to think about herself. Not much, but a little. She found herself smiling during class over something he'd said over a shared meal or while they'd watched the sunset. Her daydreaming worried her. Her classes were hard enough without a man filling her mind.

She showered and lay in bed for over an hour, winding down before she could go to sleep. Was she crazy to think she could juggle fulltime school, a job and a love affair?

She'd be lying to herself if she said she didn't want it. She wanted to continue her liaison with her sexy neighbor and looked forward to seeing him again. If it wasn't so late and she wasn't so tired, she might've sneaked over to his camper and knocked on the door. She missed his goodnight kisses and the way he wrapped his arms around her, making her feel... cherished.

She fell asleep dreaming of John lying next to her, holding her close, the sound of his heartbeat soothing her.

The next day, Collette woke with a smile, ready to face the day and night at work.

Hope was already up, dressed and ready for school. "Ryan's on his way. I'm hanging out at the library this afternoon. Mr. Sanders is giving me a ride home, and then Ryan and I are having dinner with his folks. See you later."

Collette followed her to the door. "Do I get a hug before you go?"

"Oh, yeah." Hope grinned. "I almost forgot." She set her bag on the ground, wrapped her arms around Collette and hugged her tight. "I love you, Mom. Study hard and make me proud."

Collette laughed. "Hey, that's my line."

"It was. Now, it's my turn." Hope winked. "Have a good day and don't let the drunks get sassy with you at work."

"Thanks." Collette stood in the doorway as Hope

climbed into the car with Ryan. She waved at the young man and hurried into the trailer to dress and get ready for school. The current semester was almost over. She'd be studying for final exams soon, which left little time for her to be fooling around.

HER SCHOOL DAY was long and boring. While her instructor droned on about drugs and the origins of their names, Collette followed along in her books, made notes and started work on the study guides she'd use to cram for exams. By the end of her school day, she was already tired.

Since John was picking up Hope at the library, Collette went straight to work, changing into shorts and the saloon T-shirt in the bathroom.

The afternoon was like so many others. Soldiers came in after work, hung out with their buddies, played pool and drank too much.

Hope had texted her when she'd arrived home and when she'd left again for her date with Ryan.

Collette wondered what John would do with his evening. Did he have dinner plans with friends? She found herself wishing she didn't have to work and could be out with John, getting to know the other members of his team.

On a trip back to the bar to unload empties and fill new orders, Collette balanced on one foot to give the other a break.

"You're looking a little down tonight," Red said as she pulled the tab, filling a mug full of beer. "What gives?"

"It's been a long week."

"And you'd like time off to be with your girl." Red jerked her head toward a table full of noisy young men. "Instead, you're here with a bunch of strangers, having drinks spilled on you and men asking for your number and your bra size."

Collette laughed at the absurdity and truth of her statement. "Yeah. I'm just tired, and I know I have a long way to go before my schooling is done. If not for school, I could get a job that pays enough I don't have to wait tables." She looked at her coworker and friend. "How do you do it?"

"I'm not waiting tables for one. The bar is between me and the customers. That helps. And I like what I do. Call me crazy. I get to meet new people, practice barroom psychology and work with Sarge."

"One of the perks of the job," Sarge said as he passed behind her carrying a case of whiskey.

"When do you have time to be with Blade?"

"Every night," she said. "Granted, he's asleep on the nights I work, and he has to get up in the early hours of the morning. But we make time to be together on my days off."

"That's the problem with going to school and working at the same time," Collette said. "I don't have much spare time."

"To have a life?" Red nodded. "I'll take whatever time I can get with my man, knowing he could deploy at any moment and be gone for months at a time. If you want something bad enough, you make time for it while you can. You have to grab for the joy. Nobody's going to hand it to you. It's as simple as that." She slapped a mug of beer on Collette's tray and grinned. "And you didn't have to pay a psychologist to have him tell you that. I give advice for free. I learned everything I know from the school of hard knocks and some psychology books I bought on the internet." She winked and popped the top off a bottle of beer. "You better get those drinks to that group of guys before they start tearing up the place." Red turned to a customer at the bar, smiled and joked with him.

Collette admired the woman. She was young and beautiful but had a job that kept her from being with her man. They passed each other coming and going. Yet Collette had never seen Red happier than after she'd returned from her trip to Cancun with Blade. She'd said he'd finally come to his senses and realized he loved her. She'd loved him all along but had remained in the friend zone for far too long. Now, they were together and seemed to be very happy.

The night passed without major incidents. Every time a customer came through the door, Collette looked up, hoping it would be John. As the hours passed, she quit looking and concentrated on making it to closing time. She forced smiles, laughed when she was expected to and raked in the tips that would help her buy this week's groceries. She might even have enough to replace her battery if she needed a new one. So far, her car still started, and she was able to get to work and school without getting a jump.

An hour from closing, Collette's energy level hit rock bottom. On a trip back to the bar with a tray loaded with empties, she tripped over her own feet. The tray flew from her hands, the mugs and empty bottles launching across the floor to crash into the bar.

Collette landed on her knees on the sticky floor. For a moment, she stayed there, too exhausted to pick herself up, much less clean up the mess she'd just made.

Strong arms gripped her shoulders and lifted her to her feet. Those same arms turned her around and gently held her for a long moment, pressed against a solid chest "Hey," a familiar voice whispered in her ear. Warm breath stirred the tendrils of hair that had escaped her ponytail.

She looked up into John's warm brown eyes and nearly cried her relief. "When did you get here?"

"Just now," he said.

As much as she wanted to remain in his arms, she had to clean up the broken glass and spilled liquid before someone got cut or slipped. She pushed away from him. "I'm glad you're here, but I have to work."

"Sit," he said.

Collette shook her head. "No, really, it's my job. I get paid to do the work."

"I'll take care of the this. You can take a break. You look like you need one."

When he turned to pick up the tray, Collette touched a hand to his shoulder. "John, I appreciate that you want to help, but you don't work here. I do. Let me do my job."

He straightened, a frown furrowing his brow. "I don't like to see you so tired."

"I'll be okay. We close in an hour. I can make it to then. I've done it before. I can do it again." She smiled. "The fact that you're here is enough."

He stared down into her eyes for a moment then nodded. "Okay. I'll just sit here and drink a beer. Do you mind if I at least walk you to your car when you leave?"

She sighed. "I'd love that."

For the rest of that hour, Collette felt a surge of renewed energy. With John nearby, she had incentive to make it to closing. He'd be there to walk her to her car. He might even kiss her.

Her pulse sped, and her feet didn't drag. Hell, she felt almost giddy with anticipation.

When the last customer left, John still sat at the bar.

Collette carried one last tray of mugs to the bar and slid them across to Red.

The bartender tipped her head toward John seated at the other end of the bar. "Blade said Tank had a girl." Her lips twisted in a smile. "He didn't say it was you."

Collette unloaded the tray, stealing glimpses of the man in the process, her chest swelling with warmth at Red's words. "Blade said that?"

"I didn't get the whole story, just the digest version. The guys gave Tank hell about it."

Collette's heart sank into her shoes. "Do they think I'm not good enough for him?"

Red laughed. "No. Not at all. They take advantage of every chance they can get to poke fun at each other. They're actually thrilled the old man of the unit is involved with someone. They think highly of Tank and wish him only the best." She chuckled. "They just show it in peculiar ways." Red touched her hand. "I'm happy for you both."

Collette didn't tell Red that it was news to her that she was Tank's girl. Tank hadn't made any declarations or asked her if she wanted to be in a relationship. Shouldn't she be consulted on such a personal commitment? She stared across the bar at the man who'd waited patiently for her to finish her job and had difficulty stirring up enough anger to chew him out for announcing they were a thing to his friends.

Strangely, she felt warm and fuzzy inside instead of mad. Still, he couldn't go around telling his friends he had a girlfriend before he told her.

After the floor had been swept and mopped and the tables cleaned, the chairs set to rights, Sarge declared it was time to call it a night.

Collette gathered her purse and headed for the door.

John fell in step with her, walking her all the way to her car, ducking to peer inside the window to make sure no one had stowed away in her back seat.

When he reached out to pull her into his arms, Collette planted a hand on his chest, holding him off.

He frowned. "Is something wrong?"

"I'd say so," she shot back at him. "Red said you told your buddies you have a girl. Do I know this girl?"

Tank ground out, "Blade has a big mouth."

"So, it's true?" Collette shook her head.

"Yes and no." John pushed a hand through his hair and stared out at the night.

Collette crossed her arms over her chest. "Which part is yes, and which is no?" Like his buddies, she was going to give him hell. She almost felt sorry for him.

"Yes, my friends can't keep their mouths shut, and no, I didn't tell them that I had a girl. And it's woman. Not girl. You're not a girl."

Her heart swelled. At least she was the woman he supposedly had. "Isn't it customary to notify the woman when she's considered someone's woman?" Collette demanded.

John shoved his hand through his hair one more time, looked to the night sky as if for inspiration, and then let his arms fall to his sides. "I made the mistake of admitting I was falling for someone. Rucker was the one to say I had a woman. News like that spreads like wildfire through a team. I couldn't convince them otherwise after that. All I said was I think I'm falling for someone." His voice softened, and his hands reached for hers. "You might be the last one to know, when you should have been the first. I was having a moment of confusion and needed clarity. I needed to talk to someone, and the guys—though they can be assholes—are always there to listen."

Collette didn't hear anything past his confession that he was falling for someone. Her chest tightened and butterflies erupted in her belly. "Why didn't you talk to me?"

"You didn't want a relationship."

"Neither did you." She squeezed his hands. "And yet, here we are. Two people who aren't in positions to commit—"

"Who seem destined to be together," John concluded. "I didn't want to screw it up and scare you away by saying anything so soon."

"Am I that difficult?" she asked.

"No. You're determined and driven." He pulled her into his arms. "I don't want to get in your way or derail you from succeeding."

"And I don't think I can wait four years for you to retire so we can be together."

"Deltas deploy," John said. "I might not be around much in the next four years."

Collette lifted his hand to press it against her cheek. "A wise woman once told me that if you want something badly enough, you make time for it. She also said that you have to grab for the joy in life. No one's going to hand it to you." She looked into his eyes, the glow of the streetlights reflecting in their dark depths. "When were you going to tell me how you felt?"

He shrugged. "I didn't have a plan. I was going to play it by ear. After all, we haven't known each other very long. I wanted to give you time to get used to the idea of us."

Collette chuckled. "Considering you fill my night and day dreams, I'd say I'm getting bombarded by the idea of us, to the point I can't focus on school."

John's fingers tightened around hers. "And that's exactly what I didn't want to happen. Your training is important to you and Hope. I don't want to be the one to distract you to the point you fail." He shook his head. "I never should've said anything to anyone. The time isn't right. You need your space and a clear mind. Forget what Red said. Forget that I'm falling for you. You do what you have to. I'll leave you alone." He tried to pull free of her grasp.

Collette wouldn't let go of his hands. "It's too late."

"Too late." His eyebrows formed a V over his nose.

"I know. You can't take it back, and I can't forget." She moved closer, raising his hand to her cheek again. "Nor do I want to forget. I didn't want to get involved with anyone. Not now. But we don't always get to choose when we will find that person who makes our heart sing. And, trust me, I didn't think I'd ever find him—until a certain Delta Force soldier moved his camp trailer into the park beside me and saved my daughter from a gang of druggies. I'm not sure what I'm feeling is love, but my chest aches when I'm not with you, and I think about you every hour of every day. If that's not the beginnings of love, it might be a terminal disease I won't recover from."

He raised her hands to his lips and kissed the backs of her knuckles. Then he pulled her into his arms. "For the record, I think I'm falling in love with you, Collette McCallick. You might not be the first one I told, but you're the only one who counts."

She leaned up on her toes and brushed his lips with hers. "And I might be falling for you, John Sanders. And you're right…we need to give ourselves time to get used to the idea of us. And to give Hope time as well. We may discover we're better as just friends."

John was already shaking his head before she finished her words. "Not just friends. I want you more than I've wanted any friend. I want to share sunsets with you for the rest of my life."

Collette laced her hands behind his neck and pulled him down to kiss her. "Shut up, soldier, and kiss me already."

He did, stealing her breath away in the process.

When she finally came up for air, she swayed against him. "You realize we're still in the parking lot, don't you?"

He nodded. "We should get you home. Hope will be asleep before you get there."

Collette nodded. "I'm not ready to tell her anything yet. Does that bother you?"

John shook his head. "No. Until we know exactly what we're dealing with and where we want to take this, we should keep it on the down low."

"Except for your team?" Collette said with a twisted smile.

"Except for those dumbasses." He shook his head. "They mean well, but sometimes, I want to punch them in their throats."

"If they hadn't said anything, we'd still be bumbling through the motions."

John stared down into her eyes, his own so intense. "Do you have any doubt we'd have figured it out?"

Collette shook her head. "No. But we would've wasted so much time in denial. At least, now, we can move forward and see if this works."

John waited for her to get into her car and start it before he got in his truck.

Collette led the way back to the trailer park, her heart so light and full of hope, she barely felt the ache in her feet.

She was John's woman and, if she wanted, he was her man.

A giddy feeling filled her chest.

They kissed again before she went to her trailer, and he went to his camper. With an impressionable teen in the house, Collette didn't feel right about John moving in with them. If things progressed to permanence, they'd cross that bridge when they came to it.

In the meantime, Collette needed sleep. She had chores to catch up on the next day and another hard night serving at the Salty Dog.

It was strange to go back to her old routine when that day had meant so much more.

There was nothing like a strong dose of reality to bring her back to ground. Hopefully, she and John would be able to sneak a little alone time together that weekend. Saturday morning might be an option if Hope got out early. If not, they had all day Sunday to make time for each other. She'd make the time to be with him. He was worth it.

Collette went to sleep with a smile on her face and dreaming of getting naked with John.

CHAPTER 11

JOHN WOKE early and more refreshed and rejuvenated than he'd felt in a long time. He couldn't wait to get out of bed and start the day. He went for an early morning run, came back and showered, and then cooked bacon, scrambled eggs and toast enough for three. He made sure he left his windows open so the smell might drift into the trailer next door and wake the two young women he hoped to have over for breakfast.

When the savory scents didn't do the trick, John scraped the food onto a pan and placed it in the tiny oven to keep warm. He waited another hour and, finally, walked over to knock on the trailer door.

Hope answered, wearing denim shorts and a Dallas Cowboys jersey.

"Good morning, sunshine. Is your mother awake?"

Hope nodded, a frown denting her brow. "Yes, and she's singing. Please, make her stop."

John laughed. "I have a pan full of scrambled eggs, bacon and toast at my place. Come over when you're ready."

"I'm ready," Hope said. "I'll let Mom know. Maybe she'll stop singing long enough to eat." The teen rolled her eyes. "It's just not right to be so cheerful this early on the weekend."

John chuckled all the way back to his trailer where he pulled their breakfast out of his oven and served it onto three separate paper plates.

Hope and Collette showed up as he was pouring orange juice into plastic cups.

They ate, talking about their plans for the day and evening.

John invited Collette and Hope to go with him to a home show at a convention center in Waco.

Hope shook her head. "Thanks, but I'm not at that stage in my life that home shows interest me. Now, if it was a comic convention or technical trade show, I might go." She held up her hand. "For me, it's a pass."

Collette pressed her lips together and sighed. "If I didn't have to be on my feet for work tonight, I'd go. I just can't see walking all over a convention center, and then being on my feet at the saloon." She turned to Hope. "You have the movie marathon with the youth group tonight, don't you?"

Hope nodded. "Ryan will be off work in time to take me, so I don't need a ride or the car."

"If anything changes and you need a ride home, you can call me," John said. "I'll be at one of my team-mates' houses watching the Texas A&M game on his big screen television."

Hope grinned. "I wouldn't dream of interrupting such an important game for a mere ride."

"I'll be at work," Collette said.

"I'll come over as soon as the game is over," John promised.

Collette smiled. "You don't have to do that, but I'd like that very much."

John tried again. "Can I interest either one of you in a drive out to Belton Lake? We can take a picnic lunch and fish or skip stones."

"As tempting as that sounds, once again, I'll have to pass." Hope pushed to her feet. "In anticipation of a late-night movie marathon with the youth group, I'm going to go back to bed to sleep another two or three hours." She gave her mother a pointed look. "Mom, you might consider doing the same. You look tired."

Collette touched a hand to her face. "That bad?"

"No, but you work too hard," Hope said. "You deserve a day of rest." She left the adults sitting at the table and returned to the trailer for her two or three hours of additional sleep.

Collette met John's gaze. "Would you be disappointed if we didn't go to the lake?"

John shook his head. "I would rather you caught up on your rest. You were pretty worn-out last night, and tonight will be just as hard."

"Thank you for understanding," Collette said. "If you want, you can join me. We can leave the door open so Hope will know we're not doing anything to embarrass her."

"You know that sounds better than a convention or a picnic at the lake any day. Give me a few minutes to clean up here, and I'll be over."

Collette grinned and hurried to her place.

John tossed the paper plates, washed the pans and cups and left them to dry on a dishtowel. When he was done, he locked up and walked over to the trailer.

Collette met him at the door, pressing a finger to her lips. "Hope is already asleep," she whispered.

John toed off his boots at the door and followed Collette to her bedroom.

The last time he'd been there, they'd made love into the wee hours of the morning. His cock hardened at the memory. Sadly, he wasn't there to make love to her, he was there to make sure she got some much-needed rest.

If Hope went somewhere with her boyfriend on Sunday, John hoped to get Collette alone so he could give her a deep-tissue massage all over her body. *Then* they might make love. Massage first.

Wearing a pair of soft stretchy shorts and a T-shirt, Collette crawled onto her bed, lying on top of the comforter.

John laid down beside her and reached for her hand.

For the next thirty minutes they lay that way, each staring up at the ceiling.

Then Collette rolled onto her side, tucked her hand beneath her cheek and snuggled against John's chest. A minute later, she slept.

John lay for another thirty minutes, telling himself he could handle being close to her without touching her in a sexual way.

He knew it was a lie.

The longer he lay in the bed where they'd been intimate, the more he wanted to take her in his arms and make love to her. His cock strained against his denim jeans. No matter how much he tried to think of anything else, he came back to the image of Collette lying naked beneath him as he drove deep inside her.

Swallowing a groan, John eased out of the bed and stood.

He stared down at Collette, envying her ability to go to sleep so quickly. He didn't want to wake her to let her know he was leaving. She needed to sleep and conserve her strength for another night at the Salty Dog.

To burn off the coiled energy inside, John returned to his camper, slipped into shorts, a T-shirt and his running shoes and went for a five-mile run.

When he got back, he washed his truck and prepared a lunch of chicken quesadillas.

By that time two hours had passed, he'd just flipped the last of three quesadillas when Collette appeared in his doorway, disheveled, her hair sticking out in places and her cheeks a rosy pink. "Something smells good."

The five miles he'd run didn't keep him from reacting to her all over again. His groin tightened automatically. He was so distracted by her appearance he almost burned the last quesadilla.

After scraping it out of the pan onto a plate, he turned and handed the plate to her. "If you'll carry the plates out to the table, I'll bring the condiments. Is Hope awake?"

"Not yet," Collette replied. With two plates in her hands, she descended the camper steps.

John was right behind her with salsa, a jar of jalapeños and two cans of root beer.

While they ate, they talked about the game that night and the news headlines.

"I saw that a fifteen-year-old girl went missing a week ago not too far from here," Collette said. "It worries me that Hope doesn't have a car to drive. I keep thinking I could take a bus to class and work and let her have the car."

"Between you and me, we've got her covered," John said.

"For now." She sipped her can of root beer, staring out across the farmer's field. "The problem is, you can't always be our backup. If you deploy, we'll be on our own again. Also, you're only here until your house is finished."

She was absolutely right.

He could be in another country, unable to help in any way. "But if I deploy, my truck will be here. You could use it and let Hope use the car."

Collette looked across the table at him. "You'd do that?"

He nodded. "I would."

"You're a good man, John Sanders."

"Yes, he is," Hope said as she joined them at the table and nodded toward their plates of quesadillas. "You don't happen to have another one of those, do you? They smell delicious."

John leaped to his feet, ducked into his camper and came back out with the plate he'd left warming in the small oven. He'd also snagged another can of root beer.

"Thank you." Hope took the plate, poured half the bottle of salsa on the quesadilla and topped it with jalapeños.

"Those are hot," John warned.

Hope grunted, sank her teeth into the tortilla and moaned. "Mmm. So good."

"Thanks," John said.

Hope ate in silence, polishing off the entire quesadilla before she stopped to breathe. Still chewing the last bite, she pushed to her feet. "I hate to eat and run, but Ryan should be here any minute. We're going to help set up for the movie marathon at the church tonight. We won't be back until after midnight." She tossed her plate and drink can in the trash and rubbed her hands on her shorts. "If you get off earlier, that's where I'll be. You don't have to wait up for me."

Collette exchanged a glance with John. He could tell she was worried about her daughter. She'd be awake until her daughter was safely beneath her roof.

"It'll probably be one or two in the morning before I get off," Collette said. "Text me when you get home so that I know you got here."

Hope nodded. "Will do."

The crunch of tires on gravel heralded Ryan's arrival.

"Later, Mom. I love you." Hope hugged her mother.

When she turned to give John a hug, he was too shocked by her gesture he didn't think to hug her back. "Have a good time, Hope," he said, then cleared his throat.

Collette's gaze followed Hope as she rounded the corner of the trailer. "I worry about her."

"I know." Hope wasn't his daughter, but John worried, too. Was that what being a parent felt like? He wasn't sure he wanted children of his own if he felt like that all the time. The world was a scary place.

Collette smiled at John. "Thank you for a late lunch. Like Hope, I hate to eat and run, but I'd better get my shower and get to work early. We're short staffed this evening. I'd like to get a jump on stocking the bar. Will I see you later?"

He nodded. "Yes, ma'am."

She stood, and he followed suit, going a step further by wrapping his arms around her waist and holding her for long moment. Then he bent to kiss her.

She tasted of salsa, hot and spicy.

"Tomorrow..." she said. "We're going to make time for just me and you." She clasped the back of his neck, dragged him down to her and kissed him long and hard. When she broke it off, she said, "I'll see you later."

John resisted the urge to follow her and kiss her again. They'd have time tomorrow for more of that. If he had to rent a hotel room, he'd do it to have some privacy with his woman.

With that plan in mind, he cleared the table, washed the dishes and drove over to Mac's place to watch football with his friends.

· · ·

THE NAP HAD DONE Collette wonders. She felt lighter on her feet and full of energy. It must have showed. Sarge approached her early in the evening, asking if she had more of whatever she'd taken to be so peppy.

She'd laughed and told him it had been a natural remedy called a nap.

Red noticed as well, smiling when Collette smiled every time she came to the bar to fill orders and drop empties. "I take it your man is making you very happy."

Her man.

Heat filled Collette's cheeks. "I had a nap earlier."

Red grinned. "With him, I take it. I've never seen you happier."

Collette had never felt happier. That her happiness hinged on one man was a little disconcerting and exhilarating at the same time. She'd avoided men for the past sixteen years while raising her daughter. Why was she so quick to embrace one now?

Because it was John Sanders. He was special. The man made her want to hug him all day long and keep hugging him for as long as there was life left in her.

It wasn't just the hugging... Collette had rediscovered passion, and she couldn't get enough. She found herself counting the minutes until she saw John again.

The night flew by, busier than ever with customers shouting for beer and burgers.

Collette's cheerfulness didn't wane, and the tips reflected her customers' appreciation. As midnight approached, her attention went more and more to the door in anticipation of John's arrival. The game had been over for a couple hours, the Aggies winning against Georgia. John would be in a good mood after a good game and time spent with friends.

Collette hoped she'd get to spend time with his friends, getting to know the men he considered brothers. She also looked forward to getting to know the group of women the men were dating or were engaged to. At least, she knew one of them. She glanced across the room at Red, manning the bar, providing drinks in a smooth and efficient manner.

The strawberry blonde glanced up, caught her gaze and grinned. Then her gaze shifted to somewhere over Collette's shoulder, and her grin broadened. She tipped her head toward the entrance and mouthed the words, *He's here.*

Butterflies erupted in Collette's belly as she turned to find John striding across the floor toward her.

He was so tall and ruggedly handsome he made her knees weak.

"Hey," he said as he came to a stop in front of her.

"Hey, yourself." Instinct told her to throw her arms around him, but she couldn't. Her hands were full, balancing a large tray full of beer and whiskey.

"Need help with that?" he asked, and then grimaced. "Sorry, it's habit."

She smiled. "Thanks, but I've got this."

"I'll be at the bar, keeping Red company." He leaned in and pecked her on the cheek. "You're beautiful, you know that?"

Her heart swelled with the flood of feelings she had for the man. She couldn't stop grinning as she set drinks in front of customers and took more orders.

On her way back to the bar, her cellphone vibrated in her back pocket. She set her tray on the bar, gave her order to Red and pulled out her phone to check for incoming texts.

There was one from Ryan. She frowned as she opened the text and read the cryptic message.

Ryan: Come to the church. Sly was here with his gang. We can't find Hope.

Collette's heart sank to the pit of her belly, and the blood drained from her brain, leaving her lightheaded and shaky.

An arm slipped around her, pulling her up against a solid wall of muscle. "What's wrong?" John's voice came to her as if from the end of a long tunnel.

She looked up into his eyes. "It's Ryan. Hope's missing." She handed him the cellphone.

Red pulled Collette's purse from below the counter and sat it in front of her on the bar. "Go. Your daughter needs you."

"But—" Collette looked around the crowded bar.

"We can handle this," Sarge said. "Go check out what's happening, and let us know what we can do to help."

Red had her cellphone out, dialing. "I'm calling Blade. He can get the guys rolling."

"Thanks." John's arm tightened around Collette's waist as he turned her toward the door and ushered her outside into the cool night air. He hurried her past her car and straight to his truck. Once he handed her up into her seat, he raced around to the driver's side, hopped in, started the engine and peeled out of the parking lot.

He broke every speed limit on his way through Killeen to the church. Thankfully, they didn't encounter any police. Collette was sure John wouldn't have stopped, even if they had.

What had Ryan meant that they couldn't find Hope? They had been together watching movies at the church. How could you lose someone in a church?

Then again, Sly and his gang had been there. They managed to create chaos wherever they went. Had they taken her daughter? Would they hold her hostage until Ryan's brother coughed up what he'd taken from them?

They couldn't get to the church fast enough for Collette. Deep in her gut, she knew Hope was in trouble. Big trouble. She leaned forward in her seat, praying for her daughter. Praying John wouldn't have a wreck. Praying.

Flashing lights greeted them as they pulled up to the church parking lot. A police officer blocked them from entering the church grounds. Teenagers huddled in groups. Parents who'd made it past the police officer gathered their children close.

"You can't park in here," the officer said.

Collette leaned across the console. "I'm Collette McCallick. My daughter is the one who's missing."

The officer stood at attention. "Sorry, ma'am. You can park to my right. The officer in charge is over there." He pointed to a handful of police officers surrounding what appeared to be the youth group chaperones and Ryan Alston.

Collette didn't wait for John to come to a complete halt before she flung open her door and leaped out of the truck. She ran toward Ryan, tears welling in her eyes. She couldn't cry. Not now. Hope needed her to keep her head on straight.

John caught up with her as she reached Ryan.

"This is Hope's mother," Ryan said to the men and women wearing the Killeen police department uniforms.

The officers parted, allowing Collette into their circle. She didn't stop until she stood face to face with Ryan.

"What happened?" she demanded.

Ryan's face was pale, and he had a black eye and

busted lip. "Sly and his gang. We were just leaving the church when they showed up on their motorcycles. They harassed the kids, trying to run them over with their motorcycles. Some of them made it out in their cars. I tried to get Hope to my car, but Sly blocked our path. I told her to run for it, and I stood my ground with Sly." He shook his head. "He practically ran me over. When I hit the ground, he had a couple of his guys rough me up. I couldn't see where Hope was. I thought she'd made it to the car and would be hiding behind or under it. Someone must've dialed 9-1-1 because the police came. Sly and his gang left before the cops arrived. As soon as I could, I ran for my vehicle." He raised his hands palms up. "She wasn't there." His fingers curled into fists. "I bet Sly took her, the bastard. And I don't know where to look."

"Ma'am, I'm officer Steiner. I'm in charge of this case." He held out his hand and shook Collette's. "We're doing everything we can to find your daughter. We've issued an all-points bulletin on Leon Rankin."

Collette frowned.

"Leon Rankin is Sly's legal name," Ryan explained.

The officer continued. "We've searched the building and will canvass the area for witnesses. As soon as we know anything, we'll let you know. I'll need your cellphone number and address. It would help if you went home, in case she ends up there."

Collette pressed her lips together and lifted her chin. "I'm not going home without my daughter."

Steiner nodded. "You're welcome to stay here as long as you don't interfere with the investigation." He walked away to give direction to the officers standing around.

Collette and John remained with Ryan.

"Did you see anyone go toward your truck?" John asked.

Ryan touched a finger to his busted lip and winced. "I was otherwise occupied." He pulled his cellphone out of his pocket. The screen was cracked, but the light flickered on. "I've texted my brother again and again since Sly started harassing us." He jabbed his finger at the screen, his voice tight with anger. "He should be the one dealing with this. I don't know where Sly hangs out." He looked up, his face haggard for one so young. "I don't know where to look."

"I do," a voice said behind them.

Collette, John and Ryan spun to face a young man with shaggy hair and wrinkled clothes.

Ryan froze for a moment then cocked his arm and punched the guy in the face. He winced and shook his hand.

The young man he'd hit reeled backward, steadied himself then rubbed the red spot forming on his jaw. "I guess I deserved that."

"Damn right, you did," Ryan said.

"I heard what happened and came as soon as I could."

Ryan glared at him. "If you'd come out of hiding a week ago, this would never have happened. Hope wouldn't be gone." He turned to Collette. "This is Mark, my brother."

CHAPTER 12

JOHN FOUGHT the urge to punch Mark Alston himself. As satisfying as it might have been, it wouldn't help them find Hope. "You said you might know where Sly and his gang would've taken her?"

Mark nodded, his gaze going to the group of police officers. "I can take you there, but not with them," he said, lowering his voice. "Flashing lights and uniforms will have them scattering into the woods. If they have your Hope, they'll make her disappear with them. I can get into their location because I have what they want. I never planned to give it back, in fact, I'd planned on flushing it down the drain, but thought I might use it to work with the DEA to bring Sly and his gang down. I wanted more than just the two-bit middleman drug dealer. I wanted his supplier. I was holding out until I found him." Mark shook his head. "Then I got your text, brother. I had to come out of hiding."

"Nice of you to do it now," Ryan said, his anger still palpable.

"I should've turned the drugs over to the DEA sooner. I know that now. Then Sly would've known he would never get his hands on it. He might not have targeted my family." Mark sighed. "I'm sorry. However, because I still have the package, we have something to bargain with."

John's cellphone vibrated in his pocket. He pulled it out and scanned the message. His team was parked along the street a block from the church. They were ready to help. "Come on. We may not have much time. The longer Hope's missing, the harder it'll be to find her." He didn't add the word *alive.*

He hooked Mark's arm and ushered him toward his truck. "I have a team of Deltas. We know how to infiltrate and neutralize. You provide the distraction. We'll provide the muscle."

Mark stopped beside the truck and shook free of John's grip. "We need to make a stop along the way so I can retrieve the package they want."

Ryan started to get in the back seat of John's truck and stopped, frowning. "Should I stay in case they do find Hope around here?"

Collette nodded. "We need someone here keeping tabs on what the police are doing."

Ryan nodded. "If you find her, tell her I'm sorry. I should've protected her better."

Collette hugged him hard. "You did your best. She'll know that. I'll let you know as soon as we find her."

John blocked Collette's access to the passenger side door. "I want you to stay here as well."

Collette shook her head. "If they have Hope, I need to be there."

He shook his head. "They're armed. My guys are combat trained. You aren't. We can't infiltrate the gang's compound if we're worried about you."

"You mean if *you* are worried about me." Her brow twisted. "I want to be there for my daughter."

"I want that for you too, but you'll put my guys at risk if they're too busy protecting you and not focusing on the mission and their own safety."

Collette heaved a sigh. "I get it. I'd be a liability." She nodded once. "I'll stay." She caught his arm and leaned up on her toes to kiss his lips. Then she stood back. "Go. Find Hope. Ryan and I will stay and learn what we can from the police."

Mark climbed into the passenger seat, and John got behind the wheel. He eased the truck past the cop standing guard at the entrance to the parking lot and drove out onto the street.

A block away, he found Rucker, Mac, Dawg, Lance, Dash, Blade and Bull gathered around Rucker's truck. As soon as they spotted John's vehicle, they stepped forward and waited for him to fill them in on what was going on.

Mark stood in the middle. "Sly's gang hangs out at an abandoned barn south of town. The place is overgrown and can't be seen from the road. There are trees around it that could provide cover. They guard the road going in, but not much else. Nobody knows the old barn is there. Sly's gang has used it for a couple years now and have gotten sloppy about security."

John took it from there. "We'll follow Mark to the turn off and keep going another half mile past, ditch the vehicles and go in on foot. What do we have in the way of arms?"

A quick inventory of each man's weapons yielded a handgun for all and several military knives.

John had a nine-millimeter Glock beneath the seat of his truck and a conceal carry license if he needed it. "Sly will likely be armed."

"And at least half of his gang carry," Mark added. "I can't tell you which ones."

"Then assume they're all armed," Rucker said.

"Mark's going in on foot with the drugs they want back."

Mark nodded. "I'll attempt to negotiate a trade for Hope. They might not go for it, because they'll think I'm alone and they can just take the package from me."

"Give us ten minutes before you go in so we can

get into place," Rucker said. "We'll have your back should they get stupid and start shooting."

John faced the younger man. "You don't have to do this. One of us can go in with the drugs. They might be less likely to shoot a stranger."

Mark snorted. "They have to be running scared of their dealer to have gone to so much trouble to get the drugs back. They'll be edgy and nervous." He shook his head. "No. I'll take it in. I started this. I'll finish it. For Hope and for my family. I put them through enough."

Once they had nailed down the plan, the team consolidated to three vehicles.

On the way out of town, Mark had John stop just before a bridge over a dry creek bed. Mark hopped out, disappeared down the bank and ducked beneath the bridge. A moment later, he emerged, carrying a black garbage bag. He climbed into the back seat. John took off with his team, following at a distance behind them.

Five miles down the highway, Mark had John slow the vehicle. As they passed an old live oak tree that had died due to oak wilt, Mark pointed over John's shoulder at two weathered fence posts on either side of what appeared to be an overgrown driveway, now rutted and covered in grass.

John looked closer in the light from his truck's headlights. The grass laid over where tires had smashed it down. He pulled a hundred yards past the driveway and stopped long enough for Mark to get out with his bag of drugs. Then John continued past the entrance, speeding up until he'd gone half a mile. He found another dirt road leading off the main highway and pulled into it. His team came in behind him. They dismounted and gathered their weapons. Few words were spoken. They had less than ten minutes to get in place before Mark presented himself and the prize Sly had been searching for.

The clear Texas sky full of shiny stars helped them pass through the brush quickly as they neared where they'd calculated the barn would be. They slowed their forward movement and slipped from shadow to shadow. If they could see clearly, Sly's people would be able to spot them if they stood out in the open.

Soon, the silhouette of a large old barn rose above the stubby live oak trees.

The team spread out and inched closer.

Mark had made his way down the rutted path and was just coming to the sentry, standing guard over the road in. He shouted something, and Mark stopped.

Speaking in a clear, loud voice, Mark said, "I'm here to do business with Sly. Let him know Mark's come to do him a favor."

A man standing in front of the barn ducked through the doors. Moments later, five men emerged. John could pick out Sly. He was the one with the swagger and attitude in the middle of the others. "Bring the thief here," he called out.

While the gang members' attention was on Mark and Sly, John and the rest of his team moved in from all sides, surrounding the barn. Mac, Bull and Dawg would come in from behind the barn. If there was a door back there, they'd go through it and take out any opposition along the way.

Rucker and John moved in from the east, hugging the shadows. The barn was so overgrown, bushes and small trees had grown up all around it. The team had no trouble reaching the structure without being detected.

Meanwhile, Mark held out the bag of drugs. "I'm here to make a deal with you."

"What deal?" Sly demanded.

"The drugs for the girl."

Sly crossed his arms over his chest. "How do I know you aren't just holding up a bag full of flour, powdered sugar or cow shit for that matter?"

"It's the real thing." Mark shrugged. "But if it makes you feel better, have one of your guys test it." He set the bag on the ground and pulled out a brick of tightly packed powder.

Sly leaned his head to the guy with all the piercings beside him. "Do it."

The man hurried forward, scratched off a little of the powder and touched it to his tongue. He straightened and nodded. "It's real."

"Well, we still don't have a deal," Sly said. "I can just take it, shoot you and be done with this." He raised his hand. In it was the gun he'd pointed at Collette recently.

"This is just half of it. I've stashed the rest in the woods," Mark said. "Give me the girl, and I'll give you this and show you where the rest is. If your dealer is breathing down your neck for results, you'll need every bit of the stuff."

Sly's eyes narrowed in the starlight. "I could torture the information out of you."

"That takes time. And if your guys go too far, I'll die and you won't find the other half of your stash." Mark wrapped the brick in the plastic bag and straightened. "What's it to be?"

"I don't have the girl," Sly said. "But I'll take that bag." He stepped forward, pointing the gun at Mark.

"Where is she?" Mark asked. "I'm not giving you anything until you tell me what you've done with Hope?"

"I told you. I don't have her." He laughed. "Never have. Last I saw her, she was running around that church parking lot, trying to get away from my men."

Mark frowned. "You're lying."

Sly tensed.

John motioned to Rucker. Rucker gave the hand signal for them to move in. They passed the signal down the line. When Rucker stepped out, they all moved as one, converging on Sly's gang.

Sly ran toward Mark. "Stop, or I'll shoot him."

John rushed forward and grabbed the man's hand. Sly struggled, bringing the gun down between them.

When it went off, John froze, waiting for the flash of pain that accompanied a bullet piercing his flesh. It didn't come. Sly's eyes widened, and his grip on the gun relaxed. "I'm hit," he said.

John wrested the gun from his hand as the man slipped to the ground, a red stain spreading across his side.

The rest of the gang threw down their arms and would've run off, but the Deltas had them surrounded.

"Where's the girl?" John demanded.

Every one of the Sly's gang shook their head as one.

The man who'd tested the powder spoke out. "We don't have no girl."

"Search the barn," Rucker barked.

Bull and Mac ducked into the barn. Moments later they came out. "She's not here."

"Told you," said the guy with the piercings. "We didn't take her."

John pointed his gun at the man. "Don't lie."

He held up his hands. "Ain't lying. You know how hard it is to carry someone off on a motorcycle? You can shoot me, and I wouldn't tell you no different. We didn't take her. You're wasting your time here."

The longer John stood there, the more he believed them. "We need to get back to the church."

Eight minutes later, the team and Mark were back in their trucks, heading to Killeen and the church. John slammed his foot to floor, pushing the truck as fast as it would go. "Text Hope's mother. We're on our way back. Without Hope."

They'd gathered the guns and left two of the team standing guard over them until the sheriff arrived to deal with them and the drugs Mark had left behind.

Rucker left orders with Bull and Mac to shoot if anyone so much as twitched.

When they arrived at the church. The police were packing it in. A couple of the cruisers had departed, and all the teens were gone except Ryan. Collette stood with him and another man.

John drove right into the parking lot. No one stopped him. He parked and leaped out.

Collette ran across the pavement and threw herself into his arms.

"I'm sorry," he said. "She wasn't there."

Tears soaked through his shirt. "She has to be somewhere. She can't have disappeared into thin air."

"We're missing something," he said, looking over the top of her head at the parking lot, his gaze landing on Ryan's truck at the far end of the lot. He turned to the teen. "Is that where your truck was parked when all this went down?"

He nodded. "I shouldn't have told her to run for it. It was too far."

John strode toward the truck. Ryan, Collette, and the man with her, followed.

Collette made the introductions. "This is Pastor Graves."

"I came as soon as I found out Hope was missing." He twisted his hands together. "I've never had anything like this happen at our church. It's supposed to be a safe place for our children and families."

Something about where Ryan had parked pulled at John's memory. He walked around Ryan's truck. There was an empty parking space on the very end.

"Was there another vehicle parked beside your truck?"

Ryan frowned. "Actually, yes. A white van. The one Mr. Earles drives. But I don't remember seeing him when we came out of the church or when the bikers were circling the lot."

"Is there another way out of the parking lot?" John didn't wait for an answer, he strode past Ryan's truck and noticed an impression in the grass leading away from the church to a dirt road. The dirt road led to the highway on the other side of the church, out of view of the parking lot and everyone who had been distracted by Sly's gang.

John's pulse quickened. He turned to the pastor. "What do you know about Mr. Earles?" He started toward the church. "Where does he live?"

The pastor shook his head. "Mr. Earles has been the janitor here for two years. He keeps a clean church and doesn't talk much. When he first came to work for us, he didn't have a place to live, so he slept in the church."

"Where?" John demanded.

The pastor pulled a ring of keys from his pocket and led the way into the building. He turned away from the chapel and led them through the hallways to the back of the building. He opened a door into a large room where heating and air-conditioning equipment was housed. It was also used as a storage room for cleaning supplies and yard maintenance tools.

In the far corner, a twin bed had been pushed up against the wall. Beside it was an old locker. The bed appeared clean and dust free, as if someone had made it that morning. Other than the locker and the bed, there wasn't much else.

John searched the large room. Its high ceilings were laced with pipes and electrical conduit. As he circled back to where the bed was located, he noticed the ceiling was lower in that section. He pointed to it. "What's up there?"

The pastor shook his head. "Nothing that I know of."

John walked around, looking up.

Collette walked with him. She stopped and pointed to a string hanging down between two support beams. "What's that?"

John spotted what she was pointing at. "An attic access door." He grabbed the handle and pulled down a set of folding stairs. He climbed to the top, pulled out his cellphone and used the flashlight app to illuminate the space.

His gut clenched. "Holy shit."

"What?" Collette asked. She was halfway up the stairs behind him. "What's wrong?"

He climbed the rest of the way up and helped Collette into the attic.

The room was fairly large with some old furniture and boxes pushed to the far corners. That wasn't what had his heart pounding and his stomach tied in a knot.

Lining the walls were pictures of young women. Among them were pictures of a familiar face.

Hope.

Collette gasped and pressed her hand to her mouth, her face blanching white. "Oh my God. He was stalking my little girl."

CHAPTER 13

COLLETTE HELD her hand over her mouth to keep from losing the contents of her stomach. The janitor she'd trusted with her daughter's safety was a stalker.

"He took her, didn't he?" she whispered.

"Looks that way," John said. He moved around the room, studying every detail, from the photos on the wall to the large dog crates lined up. He dropped to his haunches and peered inside. "That isn't dog hair in there," he said. "We need to get the police up here." He strode to the attic staircase. "Rucker?"

Rucker and the rest of the team had followed them into the maintenance room and to the bottom of the attic stairs. "Here. What did you find?"

"Get the police up here ASAP."

"Dash is already halfway there," Rucker called out as he climbed the steps and poked his head into the attic. When he saw what was there, he swore. He emerged into the space.

Collette had bent to look into the crates. As John had indicated, there were strands of hair in them. Long hair. One of the strands was dark, almost black. She glanced at the photos and spotted a young woman with long black hair and Asian features. Her heart pinched hard in her chest. What had happened to her?

John pointed to other things that chilled Collette. Rolls of duct tape stacked neatly beside the crates. A can full of zip-ties. On one of the metal support beams, a metal hook had been welded into the beam. Dangling from the hook was a pair of handcuffs.

The janitor had stockpiled cases of water, toilet paper and cans of soup.

"As far as I can see, there's no sign of blood," Rucker said.

Collette moaned.

"Sorry." Rucker waved around the room. "Think of that as a good sign. Maybe he isn't...hurting his victims."

John leaned over a makeshift desk with a calendar of the current month. Numbers had been scribbled on one corner of the paper and erased. He shined his light closer. "Thirty-five thousand," he murmured.

Collette leaned close, studying the same numbers. Her gaze went to a date on the calendar from two weeks previous. She read the letters "ILE" with the number "2" beneath it. What did it mean?

A yellow notepad lay on the desk beside the calendar with a pen next to it. The top sheet had been torn off in a hurry, leaving a piece of it behind. On the torn corner was the number 2.

John bent over the pad.

"What did it say?"

"Not sure." He was reaching for the pad when a voice called out behind him. "Don't touch anything."

The officer who'd been in charge of the search for Hope came up the steps. "This is now a crime scene. Everything in this room can be considered evidence. Don't touch anything, take anything or disturb the scene in any way."

Collette caught movement out of the corner of her eye.

John reached behind his back and grabbed the yellow notepad, slipping it into his rear pocket.

Something about that pad was important enough for John to disturb that piece of evidence.

Collette didn't care as long as they found Hope. She knew the statistics in abduction cases. The first twenty-four hours were critical. Hope's life was in the balance.

"What is all this?" Collette asked, drawing attention away from John.

The cop stood in front of the photos, his jaw tight.

"Did you see the article on the news about the woman who went missing two weeks ago?"

Collette nodded. "A mother of two small children. She didn't arrive at the daycare to pick them up." She remembered the story. Her heart had gone out to the children. How frightened they had to have been.

The officer pointed to the woman with the long dark hair and Asian features. "That's her."

Collette nodded toward the pictures of Hope in the Sunday school classroom, riding her bicycle and leaning against the church door with her backpack looped over one shoulder. "That's my daughter. Hope."

"We put out an APB on Mr. Earles' van. If he's on the road, we'll find him," the officer said.

"What if he's not on the road but at the airport?" John asked.

"We notified the Killeen Regional airport security to be on the lookout for a white van and a man meeting Mr. Earles' description with a teenage girl."

John touched her arm. "Come on, we need to leave the police to do their job."

"The Texas Rangers are sending in a crime scene investigator," the officer said. "We'll find your daughter."

Maybe, Collette thought, but would they find her soon enough?

Collette backed down the attic stairs. John came down next, and Rucker was last.

"Let's go," John said and strode out of the machine room, through the hallways and out of the church building.

"Where are we going?" Collette asked straining to keep up with John's longer stride.

"The airport," he said.

"The police officer said they had that covered."

"The Killeen Regional Airport." He handed the notepad to Rucker. "It's not the only one around."

"Isn't there a general aviation airport near Harker Heights?" Lance asked.

John nodded. "It's a hunch." He ran for his truck.

Collette threw herself into the passenger seat. Ryan and Mark dove into the backseat.

"What's happening?" Ryan asked.

"Mr. Earles has Hope." John said. "Ryan, do you have your cellphone?"

Ryan leaned forward, holding out the phone. "Yes, sir."

"Look up the airport with the code name of ILE." John pulled out onto the highway and turned north, heading for Harker Heights.

"Those were the letters on the calendar," Collette said.

John dug the notepad out of his back pocket and handed it to her. "What do the indentions on that pad say?"

She squinted in the light from the dash.

"There's a pencil in the glove box," John said.

"ILE is the designation for the Skylark Field Airport near Harker Heights," Ryan called out.

Collette's pulse raced as she rubbed the pencil over the indentions on the pad. One by one, the letters appeared. ILE. The number 2 was on the torn top sheet on the pad. "Two?"

John pointed to the clock on the dash. It read 1:53.

"Two o'clock." Collette leaned forward in her seat. "Can you make this truck go any faster?"

A brief smile quirked the corners of John's lips, and he pressed the accelerator to the floorboard. "Collette, call 9-1-1 and tell them you have reason to believe an abduction is taking place at the Skylark Airport."

Collette was afraid to be hopeful, but she had to be. Hope was her world. She couldn't lose her.

She wouldn't lose her.

They were on the interstate, flying at ninety miles per hour. The other members of the John's team were right behind them.

Lights flashed on the shoulder of the road, and a police car pulled out, falling in behind the line of Deltas.

Collette placed that call to 9-1-1, adding that there were three trucks headed that way at a high rate of speed to get there before the victim could be flown out. She asked them to notify the ATC as well.

John didn't slow, didn't stop. They had to get to the airport before the clock struck 2:00.

John took the exit.

Collette could see the airport on the other side of the interstate, the runway lights were lit, but she couldn't tell if there was a plane landing or taking off.

Another police car had joined the first.

As they neared the airport, Collette spotted a small aircraft on the runway. "There!" she pointed. The craft was slowing to a stop. A white van pulled out of the shadow of a hangar and raced toward the plane.

"That's the van!" Collette cried.

A chain link fence and hangars stood between them and the runway.

At the next gap between hangers, John jerked the steering wheel to the right. He crossed a parking lot, blew through the chain link fence and out onto the runway.

Three hundred yards ahead, a man carried a body over his shoulder toward the small jet. Steps were lowered, and another man leaned down to take the body.

John's headlights glanced off red hair.

Collette sobbed. "It's Hope. Oh, sweet Jesus, get there already!"

Once the man had the woman aboard, Mr. Earles started up the steps.

The man in the plane stuck his foot out the door

and shoved the janitor in the chest, sending him flying backward. He pulled the steps up, and the plane taxied down the runway heading away from John's truck.

"No!" Collette yelled.

John pushed the truck even faster, catching up to the jet and racing past it. When he was far enough in front of the plane, he jammed on his brakes and spun the wheel, turning the truck sideways, blocking the runway.

Collette ducked, prepared for impact and held her breath.

"He doesn't have enough speed built up to fly over us," John said quietly. "The pilot has two choices. He can crash into us or hit his thrust reversers." He gripped the steering wheel, his knuckles turning white.

Collette held her breath for the longest second of her life.

The plane slowed.

"He hit the thrust reversers," John said in a rush of air.

When the plane had slowed sufficiently, the pilot turned it around.

"He's not going anywhere," John said.

He was right. The other trucks filled with Deltas, along with the four police cars, blocked the runway from the other direction.

The plane came to a halt in the middle of the runway.

The police rushed the plane and yelled, "Come out with your hands up!"

The steps were lowered, and someone stepped out, hands held high, red hair flying in the breeze.

"It's Hope!" Collette shoved open her door and jumped out.

John was a second behind her, grabbing her arm. "Wait. They might be armed."

Once Hope was on the tarmac, a policeman rushed her toward a squad car and out of harm's way.

A man stepped out of the plane with his hands up, followed by two more, one being the pilot.

They were cuffed and taken away by the police. An officer climbed into the aircraft, searched for others and declared it all clear.

At that point, John released Collette. Together, they ran to where Hope stood beside Rucker's truck. Collette flung her arms around her daughter and sobbed.

Hope soothed her mother's hair back. "I'm okay, Mom. Really."

For a long moment, Collette held her daughter. When she stopped shaking, she set Hope at arm's length and studied her face. "Are you sure you're all right?"

Hope nodded. "I'm sure. I have a little knot on my

head, and I'm a little groggy from whatever he injected into me, but I'll be okay."

An ambulance arrived. Hope rejected the ride, pointing to Mr. Earles still lying on the ground. "He needs you more than I do."

"He needs to be well enough to stand trial," John stated, his jaw tight. "That man needs to rot in prison."

"Yes, he does," Hope said. "He admitted to selling a dozen women to human traffickers."

Rucker swore beside her.

"The only good news is that he kept good records of who they were and who purchased them." Hope nodded toward the janitor. "He has it all saved in a file on his phone. He was very proud of that fact. So proud he shared it with me."

"We're taking you to the hospital," Collette said. "I want to make sure you won't have any adverse effects for the drugs he gave you."

Hope sighed. "Okay. Then I want to hit the I-Hop for pancakes before we head home to bed."

Collette chuckled. "Yeah, you're going to be okay."

Hope wrapped one arm around her mother and the other around John. "Thanks for coming to my rescue." She nodded to the other Deltas. "All of you."

John leaned over and pressed a kiss to her forehead. "I like to think that if I'd had a daughter, she'd be as smart and brave as you."

Hope smiled up at him. "Are you applying for the job?"

John laughed, and then turned serious. His gaze met Collette's over Hope's head. "I might just do that. I'd be honored to get the job."

Hope hugged him. "And I'd be thrilled to call you Dad." She turned to her mother. "What do you say?"

Collette's brow furrowed. "You're doing it again," she said, a smile forming on her lips.

John gave her an innocent expression. "Doing what?"

"You know what," Collette said. "Making up my mind without asking me first."

Hope backed out of their arms and stepped closer to Rucker. "I'll just let you two figure this out on your own."

John took Collette's hands in his. "I thought it was too soon."

Collette looked down at their joined hands. "So did I. But this..." she tightened her hold on him, "feels right." She looked into his eyes, hers blurring with tears. "Do you want me to be part of your life?"

"Hey, who's doing the proposing here?"

"Oh, come on," Hope said. "Just ask, kiss and let's get pancakes."

John's Delta friends burst out laughing.

John dropped to one knee. "Okay, okay." Still holding Collette's hands, he looked up at her. "You know you have a pushy daughter, right?"

Collette chuckled, the sound catching on a sob. "I know. She's just like me."

"Must be why I love her so much." He pressed a kiss to her fingers. "I love you, Collette. I want to watch sunsets on our back porch for the rest of our lives. Are you in?"

"What kind of proposal is that?" Hope rolled her eyes. "Do I have to coach you on everything?" She stepped forward. "John, do you want my mom to marry you?"

He nodded. "I do."

"Mom, do you want to marry John?"

A grin spread across Collette's face as John rose to his feet. "I do."

"Done." Hope marched toward the truck on the other side of the plane. "Let's get pancakes."

EPILOGUE

"You couldn't have picked better weather for your housewarming party." Rucker lifted his beer in salute. "Congrats. It's amazing."

John stood at the grill, monitoring the steaks, tongs in one hand, Collette pressed against his side. "The house wouldn't have looked nearly as nice without Collette's decorating ideas." He brushed her lips with a brief kiss before turning to flip a steak over to sear on the other side.

"How is Hope doing with the drive to and from school?" Rucker's fiancée Nora asked.

"Great. I gave her my old car." Collette smiled up at John. "John insisted on getting me a newer one to get me to school."

"We miss you at the Salty Dog," Red said from her perch beside Blade on the porch steps. "You know you can come help out anytime. We can always use another redhead slinging drinks."

"Thanks. I might do that. I like the tips. But for now, I'm concentrating on school. I don't want John to think I married him so that he could take care of me. I like to pull my own weight."

"Here! Here!" the ladies said, lifting their beers high. "To independence and equality in relationships."

"And to being on top." Red winked.

"Sophia," Blade admonished, his cheeks flushing a ruddy red.

She looked at him innocently. "What? So, I like to be on top. You know you like it, too."

He pulled her into a tight hug and planted a loud kiss on her lips. "I do. But that's our little secret."

"Ha!" Dash laughed. "There are no secrets on our team."

"That's right," Blade said. "If we don't tell them, then our women will."

Red slapped his shoulder. "Who spilled the beans about John falling in love first? You."

John looked up to see Lance walking toward him from the fence they'd spent the past weekend putting up. "Here comes the last man standing."

"We really need to find him a woman," Nora said.

"Don't do me any favors," Lance said. "I like my life the way it is. I don't answer to anyone but the Army. I can go where I want, when I want, sleep in the nude and scratch whatever itches without offending anyone in my house."

Beth leaned close to Nora. "You're right. He needs a woman. We'll have to put our heads together and find him his perfect match."

"I'm serious. I don't need a woman in my life," Lance said, his eye narrowing.

"He doesn't know what he's missing," John said. He gazed into his woman's eyes, a rush of happiness washing over him. "I got a bonus when I fell in love with you."

"Hope," she said, smiling up at him.

He nodded. "She's smart like her mother."

"And smart mouthed."

"Also like her mother." He kissed her before she could protest, loving that she didn't care that he'd won that argument.

"What do you think about children?" Collette asked.

"You already know. I love Hope. She's family, and I'm thrilled that she wants to call me Dad."

"I know, but what do you think about *small* children?"

He frowned. "What do you mean what do I think? Kids are great."

"I'm glad you think so," she said and pulled a plastic stick out of her pocket, holding it up for him to see. "You're about to find out what it's like to have one."

"Is that…? Are you…?" He dropped the tongs, picked Collette up and spun her around. "Woot! Did you hear that? We're going to have a baby!"

Hope stepped out on the porch, carrying a tray with glasses and a pitcher of lemonade. She smiled. "You told him."

Collette smiled as John set her back on her feet. "I did. I think he's not very happy."

"I'm not. I'm ecstatic. When?"

"Eight months. Early summer."

His smile turned down. "Will you have finished your training?"

She tipped her head. "It'll be close, but I think so."

"You have to finish. You've worked so hard to be a nurse."

She held up her hand. "I promise, I will."

"I can learn how to change diapers. I'm good at staying awake all night. The only thing I can't do is breastfeed."

Laughter sounded all around him as his team gathered around to congratulate him.

John only burned two steaks, but it was worth it. He was going to be a father for the second time in his life.

After everyone had gone home and Hope had gone out with Ryan, John settled on the porch swing with the woman he loved and held her hand as they watched the sun set.

"I dreamed of sitting on this porch with someone

special," he said. "Someone I wanted to spend the rest of my life with. I never believed dreams could come true. But here we are."

"Funny," she said. "I had a different dream…" She turned to him, a wicked smile on her face.

"Oh, yeah?" He cupped her cheeks and pressed a kiss to her lips. "What was it about?"

"It had to do with you and me and getting naked." She pushed to her feet, took his hand in hers and cast one last glance at the sunset. "Last one in bed and naked has to be on the bottom." She darted for the door.

John moved a little slower without being too obvious. He liked when she was on top. He'd never tell her, though.

BREAKING DAWN

HEARTS & HEROES BOOK #1

New York Times & *USA Today*
Bestselling Author

ELLE JAMES

BREAKING Dawn

New York Times & USA Today Bestselling Author

ELLE JAMES

CHAPTER 1

Sergeant First Class Lance Rankin strode toward the two Black Hawk helicopters, rotors turning, on the tarmac at an Israeli airbase near Jerusalem. Having just arrived in the country to augment a special mission, he hefted the bag containing his submachine gun and ammo. He leaned close to his Delta Force counterpart, who'd been in the country longer than him, to receive the briefing he'd hoped to have *before* they moved out.

"Glad you made it," Master Sergeant Ketchum yelled over the noise of the engines. "We'll have to brief you on the way. Intel indicated that our target will be moved to an undisclosed location tomorrow. It's now or never if we want to get him out."

"Give me the details," Lance said.

Ketchum nodded and continued toward the aircraft. "You'll be working directly with Mika Blue of the Israeli Defense Force, who's part of the point team. Once the team breaches the building, you and Blue will grab the target and get him to the extraction point. Blue is a skilled fighter and can interpret."

"Who is our target?" Lance asked.

"I'll brief you once we're all on board. For now, meet the Deltas. I'm going to check on the other members of our combined team." Ketchum turned and hurried back the way they'd come.

Lance climbed into the Black Hawk and settled on the bench beside another Delta Force operative balancing a sniper rifle between his knees. He wore a black armored vest loaded with numerous magazines and a couple of hand grenades. He gave Lance a chin lift and held out his hand. "Gonzo."

Lance shook his hand. "Lance Rankin."

Gonzo frowned. "Call sign?"

Lance shrugged. "Lance."

"No nickname?" The man's eyes narrowed as he studied Lance, his gaze taking in the scar next to Lance's left eye. "We'll have to fix that. How about Scar, Phantom or Freddy?"

Lance's lips twisted. "Or Lance or Rankin."

Gonzo shook his head. "What do you like to do when you're not out playing Army?"

Again, he shrugged. "I like to hike, run and build computers."

"How about Hiker or Runner?" Gonzo suggested.

"Or Hack..." the guy across from his said.

"Hack, it is," Gonzo grinned. "Welcome to the team, Hack."

Though he was "on loan," Lance would be a part of this unique team organized to perform a dangerous extraction. That had been all the information he'd been given before he'd left Fort Hood less than twenty-four hours ago. He'd been assured he'd be briefed once he had boots on the ground in Israel.

The man seated on the other side of Gonzo leaned forward, hand outstretched. "Bass."

Lance shook his hand and the hands of the other two Deltas seated across from him.

"Smoke," the one who'd suggested Hack was the smaller guy of the two, wiry and rugged.

Gonzo tipped his chin toward him. "He likes to pop smoke whenever he can. Likes a dramatic entrance."

The guy beside him was tall and lean. "Ice."

"On account of he doesn't get flustered when shit hits the fan," Smoke said.

"He keeps so cool, you'd get frostbite if you touched him," Gonzo added.

"Whatever," Ice said. "They tell you anything about this mission?"

"Not yet."

Ice snorted. "Gonna be a shit show."

Lance didn't like the sound of that. "How so?"

Smoke jabbed Ice with his elbow. "Let Ketchum give him the low down."

"Yeah," Gonzo said. "Let Ketchum." He nodded toward the man headed their way. "Here comes the rest of the team."

Ice snorted again. "Good thing the other Hawk is filled with more Deltas."

"How did we get stuck in this one?" Ice asked.

Gonzo grinned. "Hand selected for our skills, no doubt."

As the soldiers neared the helicopter, Lance's brow furrowed. One was shorter than Ketchum and appeared to be a lightweight, seeming too small to carry a rifle, ammo and wear an armored vest. "Are we teaming with a kid?" Lance asked.

"Worse," Ice said through gritted teeth.

"Woman," Smoke said, his tone flat, his lips pressing into a thin line.

"Hey." Gonzo glared at them. "Those soldiers, male and female, have as much or more combat time than either one of you. They're highly decorated in the Israeli Defense Force and members of the Sayeret Matkal—the equivalent of our Delta Force. So, don't judge one of them based on her gender. She earned her rank."

Ketchum and the five members of the IDF climbed on board. Ketchum directed the woman to take the seat beside Lance. Sliding onto the bench across from her, the Master Sergeant leaned forward. "Lance Rankin—"

"It's Hack," Gonzo interrupted. "For the purpose of this mission, he'll be Hack."

Ketchum nodded. "Hack…" He tipped his head toward the woman. "Meet Mikayla Blum."

She held out her hand, her lips twisting. "For the purpose of this mission, call me Mika Blue. Nice to meet you." Her voice was firm and her English perfect, with no hint of an accent. American English.

He took her small hand in his, surprised at the strength of her grip, despite her soft skin. All the while, he shook her hand, he couldn't help thinking, *Holy shit, we're going into enemy territory with a female.* Some men viewed females on the battlefield as bad luck. Two members of the team he'd be working with had already voiced their displeasure.

Now, Lance understood why he'd been hand-picked for this mission.

Mika lifted her chin and met his gaze head-on. "I understand you fought against ISIS alongside an all-female Kurdish militia."

He nodded. "I did. They were some of the bravest and most fierce fighters I've had the honor of serving with."

Ice cursed.

Smoke muttered, "You could have said something."

Lance ignored them and focused on the woman who'd take point with him. "Been a member of Sayeret Matkal long?" he asked.

She nodded. "Long enough. Over four years." Her gaze left his as she checked her gear. A moment later, she looked up and pinned him with her brown-black gaze. "Have you been a member of Delta Force for long?"

He fought a grin. "Eight years and some change." He liked that she wasn't backing down or letting him off lightly. As a female fighter in an elite force in a part of the world where men believed a woman's place was in the home, she had to have dealt with a great deal of flak from her male counterparts.

Fortunately, his experience with the female militia had changed his attitude about women in combat. He'd still felt protective of them, but no more so than other members of his team. Well, maybe a little more protective. Some of them had left children at home with grandparents while fighting to drive ISIS from their country. Still, he'd never been on an extraction mission with women as part of his team.

Ketchum leaned toward Lance. "We've been tasked to rescue and return Deputy Defense Minister Efraim Yaron. Hamas captured him while he was on a diplomatic visit to Lebanon."

Ketchum pulled out a computer tablet, tapped the screen with his finger and brought up a satellite image. "He's being held in the ruins of a bombed-out Palestinian village. Intel in the sky and on the ground indicates he's in the only building that remained intact. Here." He pointed at the screen where a white square of a building stood on the edge of the crumbled bricks and shells of those less fortunate structures.

"We'll land on the other side of this ridge from the village and go in on foot. Once we have Yaron, the choppers will meet us here." He pointed to a clearing not far from the building. "We anticipate twenty-five to thirty Hamas soldiers in attendance. Our team of twenty will move in, subdue the guards, clear the building and retrieve Yaron." He glanced up. "Questions?"

"Are they equipped with anti-aircraft weapons?" Lance asked.

"They have access to rocket-propelled grenades they've used in the past to target Israeli gunships. Whether they have them in the village, we don't know."

Lance nodded. "So, we assume yes, for planning purposes." He reached for the tablet and studied the terrain leading from the ridge to the structure where Hamas allegedly held Yaron. He frowned and pointed at a rock bluff behind the building. "Is that a drop-off?"

Ketchum nodded. "Intel on the ground estimates it's a two-hundred-foot cliff. Bravo Team, that's us, will get into position along the ridge and wait until Alpha Team circles around that cliff and establishes a perimeter surrounding the village. They will move in to tighten the perimeter to make certain no one alerts Hamas or enters the village while we're conducting our extraction. Once they're in place, we'll rappel in, take out the guards, clear the building and extract the diplomat."

Lance zoomed in on the terrain. The two-dimensional image did little to indicate how steep the hill was on either side of the cliff or any potential drop-offs that might be hidden from the satellite cameras by trees or other vegetation. Lance liked it better when they practiced maneuvers before executing them. With Hamas scheduled to move Yaron the next day, they didn't have time for such luxuries.

He turned to Mika. "Have you ever rappelled?"

She nodded. "I have. I've trained others as well."

"We have everything we'll need to get to the bottom of that cliff. It's the fastest, quietest way in. We'll take out any rear guards using rifles with silencers." Ketchum nodded toward Gonzo. "Gonzo is one of our best snipers. He'll cover us from the ridgeline."

The team performed a communications check while in route, ensuring all radios were functioning and on the same frequency. The IDF fighters had all been equipped with radio headsets similar to those used by the Deltas.

Lance checked and double-checked his rifle, pistol, gear and ammo. In his peripheral vision, he noted Mika doing the same. Once she was finished, she sat staring out the side door of the Black Hawk, her rifle resting across her knees, pointing out the door.

A dozen questions simmered in Lance's mind as he studied the woman who would be his partner, storming the building and freeing the Israeli diplomat. Chit-chat was held to a minimum, with the noise of the helicopter engines and rotors roaring in their ears. At the same time, the aircraft ate the distance between the airbase and their landing zone deep in Palestinian territory.

What felt like hours later, the helicopters slowed and lowered.

Lance's pulse quickened, and adrenaline surged through his system.

Game time.

ABOUT THE AUTHOR

ELLE JAMES also writing as MYLA JACKSON is a *New York Times* and *USA Today* Bestselling author of books including cowboys, intrigues and paranormal adventures that keep her readers on the edges of their seats. When she's not at her computer, she's traveling, snow skiing, boating, or riding her ATV, dreaming up new stories. Learn more about Elle James at www.ellejames.com

Website | Facebook | Twitter | GoodReads | Newsletter | BookBub | Amazon

Or visit her alter ego Myla Jackson at mylajackson.com
Website | Facebook | Twitter | Newsletter

Follow Me!
www.ellejames.com
ellejamesauthor@gmail.com

Lucas (#3)

Beau (#4)

Rafael (#5)

Valentin (#6)

Landry (#7)

Simon (#8)

Maurice (#9)

Jacques (#10)

Brotherhood Protectors Yellowstone

Saving Kyla (#1)

Saving Chelsea (#2)

Saving Amanda (#3)

Saving Liliana (#4)

Saving Breely (#5)

Saving Savvie (#6)

Saving Jenna (#7)

Saving Peyton (#8)

Saving Londyn (#9)

Brotherhood Protectors Colorado

SEAL Salvation (#1)

Rocky Mountain Rescue (#2)

Ranger Redemption (#3)

Tactical Takeover (#4)

The Billionaire Replacement Date (#8) coming soon

The Billionaire Wedding Date (#9) coming soon

Cajun Magic Mystery Series

Voodoo on the Bayou (#1)

Voodoo for Two (#2)

Deja Voodoo (#3)

Cajun Magic Mysteries Books 1-3

The Outriders

Homicide at Whiskey Gulch (#1)

Hideout at Whiskey Gulch (#2)

Held Hostage at Whiskey Gulch (#3)

Setup at Whiskey Gulch (#4)

Missing Witness at Whiskey Gulch (#5)

Cowboy Justice at Whiskey Gulch (#6)

Boys Behaving Badly Anthologies

Rogues (#1)

Blue Collar (#2)

Pirates (#3)

Stranded (#4)

First Responder (#5)

Silver Soldier's (#6)

Warrior's Conquest

Enslaved by the Viking Short Story

Conquests

Smokin' Hot Firemen

Protecting the Colton Bride

Protecting the Colton Bride & Colton's Cowboy Code

Heir to Murder

Secret Service Rescue

High Octane Heroes

Haunted

Engaged with the Boss

Cowboy Brigade

An Unexpected Clue

Under Suspicion, With Child

Texas-Size Secrets

Made in the USA
Monee, IL
02 November 2024

69164042R00144